A View of the Edge of the World

A Collection of Short Stories

SEAN McBRIDE

iUniverse, Inc.
New York   Bloomington

A View of the Edge of the World
A Collection of Short Stories

iUniverse books may be ordered through booksellers or by contacting:

iUniverse
1663 Liberty Drive
Bloomington, IN 47403
www.iuniverse.com
1-800-Authors (1-800-288-4677)

ISBN: 978-1-4502-4461-9 (sc)
ISBN: 978-1-4502-4460-2 (ebk)

Library of Congress Control Number: 2010910390

Printed in the United States of America
iUniverse rev. date: 08/10/2010

We Proud, We Few

I am Private James Riggio of San Francisco, California. I was enlisted in the United States Marines at the age of nineteen and have dutifully served out two years of service. I spent six months in the brig for drunk and disorderly conduct, reduced from a charge of attempted murder. I am using this journal not only to commemorate what and who I was but also as a hope that whoever finds this journal will know I was the last to survive.

The Dark came on September 23, 2012. I was aboard the transport ship *Titan* on my way to Fallujah as a refill for the casualties we were acquiring in Iraq. Front-line duty.

War is hell. It has been said before, and I echo that sentiment now. I was taken out of my normal life (we all were) and thrust into a mechanical existence. We ate when told. We slept when told. We even pissed and shit when told. They said they were training us, getting us ready for what we were going to see. They said if we didn't listen we would die. They were wrong.

The two hundred men and women aboard that transport were terrified. We knew the war had run beyond our control, and we also knew we were replaceable; we were there to replace those who had been killed, for God's sake. Our lives were so different from the carefree drama of high school. We were young and stupid, but we'd become young and deadly and scared shitless because of what lay before us.

On the fourth night aboard our frigate, at 7:00 PM, the sun disappeared. I was down below deck with Johnny C. (John Carvecchio, if you could pronounce the last name, which only a handful of us could) playing cards, losing as usual. When the Dark hit it was rumored that Capt. Luddy went to his cabin, took out his Good Book, and began to pray, leaving command to Lt. Vasquez. Vasquez promptly ordered the boat stopped so we wouldn't crash into anything. People argued later that his decision was bad, considering we were in the middle of the ocean without anything on the radar. But really, where would we have gone?

Johnny and I carried on for at least a half an hour before the intercom buzzed that we were all to get dressed and report to the deck.

We were in the room with twenty others all feeling equally lazy. Life on a ship can do that to you, even when it's only a couple of days. You're there on a ship with more than a hundred men, all equally nervous and bored. There is little room, so the thought of exercising goes right out the porthole. You sit and wait for your shift to start, talking about the same things to the same people, either lying in bed or sitting in a chair. You get so tired you can't think.

When we got up on deck Lt. Vasquez was yelling, and it was pitch black. He had a torch, of all things. A torch! PFCs Roberts and Kanon had flashlights, and every light on deck was lit up like Christmas; but the dark still pushed in on us.

"*Listen up, troops!*" Lt. Vasquez yelled. "*Get in formation and shut up!*" He waited a few seconds for us to comply, and once we did, his voice dropped significantly. "Something big has happened. Now we can sit here and whine about our plight, or we can do something about it! I got hold of the mainland, and they said that the same thing happened there: the sun has gone away. There is no intel on the matter, so we don't know if it's something the terrorists did, or if it's something cosmic."

He stopped for a moment. I looked into his eyes through the flickering light of his torch, and I saw fear. I gained respect for the man in that instant, because his captain had gone, and he stood there in an impossible situation and took charge. That took balls.

"This catastrophe has nothing to do with our main objective, however. We are on this boat to back up our fellow troops in Iraq, and that's what we're gonna do! Now do I hear any objections?"

"Yes!" It was Flattop Sam, and he looked like he just shit his pants.

"What did you say, private?" Lt. Vasquez got in his face. "You think I don't know how to make a decision? You think you can do better?"

"No, sir! I think we are in end times, sir! I think we should wait here for the judgment of God!" Flattop Sam reached up and took hold of the St. Christopher medal that hung around his neck.

"Well, I'll be damned, private. You might have a spine after all, but I wasn't askin'. *Do you see any horsemen around? Are you the Second Coming? I don't fucking think so!* Sergeant, take this bastard down to the brig!"

Lt. Vasquez turned his back to the rest of us and looked out over the water. When he spoke he didn't turn.

"Gentlemen and ladies, these are not end times; this is not Armageddon. And if you believe otherwise I suggest you keep your mouth shut, or you'll end up with Private Flathead in the brig!

"Y'all have nothing to fear. God would never hurt the corps, and you all know that; so get the fuck over yourselves!"

He turned, and I couldn't tell if the fire I saw was burning in his eyes or if it was reflected from the torches.

"Your captain is indisposed, so I'm calling the shots. Let it be known that these are my decisions and mine alone. We will be continuing on our course with the use of our instruments on board. Electricity still works, so go about your duties like you would've before. Nothing has changed. We still need to help our brothers and sisters in Iraq. Dismissed!"

He stood and watched us filter back under the deck, the fire in his eyes still blazing. He was the best leader I ever had. It was too bad he didn't last longer.

Those of us who were on duty went back to it, and those of us who weren't went back underneath. Johnny and I took up our game again, and life seemed to go on as normal. But there was something sinister in the cabin with us—something palpable. I could feel anger radiating in the room, and when I looked into Johnny's eyes I could see that he could as well.

"What the fuck, man?" It was Denise Ramirez who started the mutinous rebellion. "How the fuck could he lock up Flattop like that? Where the hell's the captain?"

Ramirez looked around the room, pausing slightly as she peered at each one of us, gauging our responses. She got to me and saw fear and guilt in my eyes; I think I might even have looked down, breaking the eye contact. It took a few more minutes before anyone spoke.

"So what are you gonna do about it?" Donny Johnson said from the corner with a gung ho look on his face, a perfect imitation of James Dean.

"I say we confront the lieutenant. I mean, what happened to Capt. Luddy? How do we know there hasn't already been a mutiny led by Lt. Vasquez?"

I wanted to remind her that the sun had just disappeared, that there might be more pressing issues ahead of us than worrying about upsetting the command line, but I kept my mouth shut. I like to think that, if we had stayed united, what happened wouldn't have, but in reality we were scared animals in a metal cage. At some point we were gonna end up at each other's throats.

Donny Johnson shook his head and broke the silence again.

"I don't think you have to worry about that. You would've heard something if the captain had been ousted. Things like that just don't happen quietly. We need to let the lieutenant do what he's doing and fall in line."

The room was dead quiet when Johnson finished. It seemed Ramirez was just feeling things out, trying to find someone who would join her cause, but once she met up with resistance she backed off.

But the work was done. Everyone in our cabin felt it—that terrible action, once voiced, almost seemed like a possibility now that the sun had gone away. The *sun* had gone away! This wasn't just some terrorist act. The LT could say anything he wanted, but we knew the truth. You can't take away a constant and say it was all a lie. This was not a normal event. This would change the way the world existed—hell, it was happening already just aboard this small frigate.

We spent a few more hours in silence below deck, reading, playing cards, or just lying in our bunks; but eventually the time came, and we went on duty. It was a relief for most of us because the cabin had become stuffy and seemed infinitesimally small now that it was packed with all those personalities.

I loved being on duty. You got to look out over that great blue expanse, moving gently, swaying in a chaotic blend of beauty and terror. There was nothing better in the world. But now there was nothing. I could feel the movement of the ocean, and through what light we had, I could see the water rippling—but it was like seeing through ink. It was such complete, utter darkness it almost made me sick. It wasn't night. There was no moon. I could see no sky. If I put my hand in front of my face I couldn't see it unless I put a flashlight to it.

I suppressed my nausea and stood guard. I could still feel the wind blowing against me, and I could feel the slight mist of the spraying water; so I acted like I was blind. I *felt* for everything, and it ended up being more valuable than trying to see—though it was slower.

Eventually my shift ended, and I went back below deck and joined the other bunch, hoping that they'd be more at ease now that they had had some time to cool down. But the opposite seemed to be true. There was tension in the air, almost like static, and instantly I wanted to be back up on the deck. I could feel fear and impatience creeping up my throat like bile, but I swallowed them down, crawled into my bunk, and listened to the silence in the room. We slept with the light on that night.

We all slept longer than we were supposed to—all except Ramirez, who didn't sleep at all. I can only imagine the schemes she thought up that sleepless night.

When I woke, the previous day felt like it had been a dream, and there beneath the soft glow of the florescent light I felt calm. I was sure that I'd go up on deck and everything would be back to normal, the sun shining brightly as we passed Sicily. The captain would be back, and we would get to Fallujah. Hell, maybe the war was already over. One could hope at least.

We all dressed in silence, one person rising from his bunk after another, until we were all up and dressed and sitting around in the common room. It could've been a normal day, one like any other, but you could see in everyone's eyes that they weren't prepared to go up on deck and check for the sun. Such an odd thing to worry about, wondering if the sun would be up.

Without saying a word, I slowly got up and walked toward the door. I knew the truth, but I had to suspend disbelief. I simply had no other hope. So I left my fellow crewmates and made my way up the stairs, hoping to catch a glimmer of that shining beauty, that golden orb of wealth. But when I reached the hatch, I was greeted with cold, black air.

A terrible truth hit me when I opened that door. The world had gone black. Gone black and *cold*. It seemed to be even colder now than before, although I guess that makes sense. If you take away the source of all that energy, you are left with merely nothing.

How cold was it going to get?

I shut the door, tried to shut my mind, and went back down to join the others.

"Still dark?" Johnny asked.

I didn't have the courage to open my mouth—I was afraid of what might come out of it if I did—so I merely nodded. I walked back over to my spot across from Johnny and began to shuffle the cards. I got through two shuffles and was about to deal when the lights went out.

"What the fuck!" It was distinctly Ramirez. It seemed that it might not have been the rabble-rouser in her that had wanted to act against Lt. Vasquez; she just couldn't keep her mouth shut.

I sat still in the horrible darkness and felt the engines of the ship come to a halt. We all sat in silence, except for heavy breathing, and waited for the lights to come back on. Perhaps it was just a short. I mean, no one knew; it could've been anything. We sat for what could only have been about ten seconds, and then I heard a soft "Oh fuck, oh fuck, oh fuck," repeated in rapid progression. I could hear the terror in that voice. He was a second away from panicking, and I could do nothing about it. I couldn't recognize the voice, and I couldn't tell where the crying was coming from; so I just sat there praying he would hold it together.

"Thank fucking Christ!" A small flame erupted in the middle of the room, and I saw the panicked face of Ramirez hunched over a Zippo lighter. Her statement seemed perfect; it succinctly conveyed the sentiment we all felt. The electricity went out, but could there still be fire? Could there still be light?

Despite her discovery, terror still hung in the air. It *was* still possible the lights had just blown, that someone would get them working again—and *soon*—but just one glance outside gave truth to the gravity of the situation. We would never have light again.

"Ohfuckohfuckohfuckohfuck." The panicked voice continued on throughout the discovery, pausing only slightly when the Zippo flame burst into existence. The timbre of the voice rose and sped, making it readily apparent that whomever it was was gonna blow a gasket.

It all happened within a matter of about a minute, between the lights going out, the panicked voice, and Ramirez striking up her Zippo. Just one short minute until we acquired our first casualty.

The panicked soldier sped from the room, screaming as he did so, his breath coming in long, gasping strides. I could feel wind blow by me as he charged. The port door crashed open, and footsteps clacked on each stair. I heard the hatch to the deck open and more panicked screaming, and then, very faintly, a crash of water.

"*Man overboard!*" I heard someone yell.

There was the clamoring of a few bodies trying to get up the stairs and screaming from above deck. I heard three more distinct splashdowns and more ambient splashing. No one ever got back on board.

In the bustle Ramirez's Zippo went out, leaving us once again in the dark. I sat, not moving, just staring off into the blackness, hoping, *praying*, that I was dreaming.

It took about five minutes for Lt. Vasquez to mobilize everyone onto the deck for a head count. The initial group that panicked all seemed to take their own lives, trying to swim for land rather than stay in our metal casket.

On deck the lieutenant was able to create makeshift

torches, which he lined in strategic places around the deck to keep it steadily lit.

"Listen up! I don't want any more panicking. We are obviously in quite a situation, but we have to take this as we would anything else. I want everyone to take any spare undershirts they may have, strip their bedding, and sleep on springs. You are to make at least five torches apiece. Is that understood?" He paced, but when no one spoke he continued. "You are not to light a torch if you are in a room with another lit torch. You are not to light a torch if you are within one hundred feet of another torch. If you come within these parameters, the person who enters must put out his torch. With expediency, people! We don't know how long we're going to be out here, so I need your complete cooperation if I'm going to get us out of this. Is that understood?"

I stood in silence, relishing the soft light of the torches. I took away the memory of the colors, the dark gray of the metal, the tans and whites of the clothes. I still remember them, however faded and convoluted the image may be. I still remember those colors, but what I remember better was the bright red splash of blood on the front of Lt. Vasquez's uniform.

"Blasphemer!" Capt. Dick Luddy burst out from his cabin storming at the lieutenant.

"Captain, please, go back to your cabin. We have everything under control." Lt. Vasquez only raised an arm at the captain, never even looking at him.

"No, you don't. This is the will of *God*!"

I remember the captain's eyes. Their feral stare, never blinking, filled with madness. I remember the crack of the gunshot and seeing Lt. Vasquez fall backward, blood pouring from a hole in his chest.

Panic ensued. I think a couple of people rushed the captain, while some ran below deck and yet more jumped over the side. I hid. I scuttled away into the dark and hid. Don't think of it as cowardice; think of it as survival.

The captain shot and killed two others before he was brought down by three brave soldiers. Everything electronic had gone along with the sun, but guns didn't run on electricity—they were mechanical. Our comforts were taken away from us, but not our weapons. Give a blathering idiot a gun, and he becomes a deadly blathering idiot.

There was screaming and crying. I remember hoping that Johnny wasn't in the fray. Soldiers were killing each other to get on lifeboats, throwing each other off the side of our frigate.

It was unbelievable how quickly they all turned on one another. They killed and stole from one another for no reason. It was like being in a riot, with the false pretense of the Dark as the reason they lashed out at one another.

Twenty minutes later I was sure all the lifeboats had been deployed, having heard them crash into the water. I tried to keep to the darkest corners, scuttling around like a cockroach, staying away from my shipmates, knowing that confrontation would only end badly. But when there are that many people on a boat, there are only so many places to hide. The battle continued to rage, but I had secluded myself from it. I couldn't even see the ambient glow of the light from all the torches on the deck. I was surrounded by the all encompassing Dark.

I was there, trying to become one with the metal of the ship, when I heard flint striking steel. A small light burst into existence, bathing me in its soft glow, revealing the crazed face of Ramirez. Somehow she had separated herself from the rest and happened to come right to me.

"Ramirez, sit down here. Save your light! Let this craziness pass, and when it's calmed down, let's join back up with the others."

I don't know if she could see my face. I assumed so, and I hoped I could display my terror and empathy.

She never responded. Instead her face contorted beyond measure, her mouth dropped open, and she let out a bloodcurdling scream. She dropped the light and grabbed for her gun. I didn't know what else to do. I charged her. I knocked her overboard and listened for her splashdown.

In the war on terror that was my one casualty, my one kill—friendly fire.

The fight gradually died down, leaving me alone in the darkness. I haven't been able to find anyone else since then. I hope Johnny got off and got to land. I hope someone comes and gets me. I hope the sun will come back.

Everyday I search the boat for others. I have to believe that others stayed—that others are alive. That I'm not alone in the Dark. The search is slow without light; but in my fight with Ramirez, she dropped her Zippo, and after two days of searching, I found it. This is how I write now, by the light of a Zippo.

If there truly is anyone left alive on this boat, we are among the dead and forgotten. The world has moved on, and there is nothing else but us, floating here in our unforgiving metal belly of a whale.

The Zippo is running out of fluid now. This is the end whether I like it or not. It has been so long since the sun left that I have no idea how much time has passed, but when I feel my face there is a beard there. The mess hall was scavenged, and I have finished what is left of the food, so now I look to the sea. I look to escape from this metal belly. If there are people on this boat, the world has become too large, for I cannot find them. I long for human interaction, and I have nothing left on this boat. I have to believe there is another way. There may be sun back in America, and I just need to get back there. The only way is through the sea.

If someone finds this, know that I survived. Private James Riggio, who got in a bar fight when drunk and beat the shit out of my commanding officer after he told me I would die in Iraq because I was weak. *I* survived. *I* made it. And if I made it this far, I'll find a way. I'll find light.

Carol-Ann and the Nothing Man

He knew Carol-Ann was outside, and it terrified him. He sat in his little hotel room staring blankly at his computer screen. He had spent months, in intervals, sitting in hotel rooms trying to finish his masterpiece, and Carol-Ann hated it. She always grilled him about it. "Why do you have to go out? What's wrong with writing at home? What do you do? Do you sleep there?"

The last question always baffled him because she always asked it. Granted there were times when he left the hotel to come home and sleep in the same bed with her, but most times he slept in the hotel room. The real reason she asked was because her jealousy had overtaken her. Carol-Ann was normally very levelheaded, so much so that people often thought she was on medication. She would sit and listen while someone would criticize her style or her paintings. She would purse her lips slightly and nod, accepting and cordial. But when it came to her man, she would lose it. She never told him the real reason because she knew she was being ridiculous, but whenever he went away she could see him sitting there in that depressing little hotel room (in her mind it was always dark and dirty; there was always only one light in the room, always stains on the walls, and always some cheap girl in a tiny pleather skirt) with a guilty and sullen look on his face while some hooker sucked his dick.

She had called him twenty minutes earlier to tell him she was coming. He was in the same position as he always was: slumped over the laptop, with one hand on his cheek and the other scratching his head, a look of consternation on his face. He came to the hotel to write. His initial reasoning seemed to make sense to him. It was full of rhythm and superstition, and it worked.

He was on the biggest tour of his career. His first book was called *Bird's Release*. It was a story from the perspective of a boy with autism, and it told of his struggles to be understood. It was pure schlock, but people loved it. The *San Francisco Chronicle* had said he "caught the breadth and possibility of life," and according to *Newsweek*, it was "pertinent and intelligent. A must-read for anyone with a soul." He saw it for what it really was: gimmicky and trite. He felt like a sell-out, as if he didn't know how to create, so he followed formulas.

His second book, *The Correct Ideal for a Failing Marriage* held a mirror to his life. This time the *Chronicle* had said he was "genius," and *Newsweek* had dubbed him a "rock star Philip Roth." The narrator of the book was a disillusioned basketball coach who spent long periods away from home—writing in hotels. In the book the couple broke up and got back together on the wife's deathbed, years later. In real life the couple ignored their problems and stayed together.

The biggest was the third. He had a large tour in New York, hitting eight stores, and he had stayed at the Hilton for a week. It was called *The Devastated Sole*, and it was about a man traveling from coast to coast trying to understand his purpose in the world. It was about that time that he started noticing a common theme entering his writing that he hadn't before: travel.

The time he spent at the Hilton in New York had been the most productive of his life, and he began to think his problems came from restlessness and being tied down. He equated this wanderlust with his inability to be happy with his home life. Namely Carol-Ann. After his tour had finished, he thought back to that room where he'd had the revelation, that place where he had been *so* productive. He thought about the joy in getting back to the room at the end of each day and pressing that power button and having that little machine show the extension of his mind as it crept out through his fingers. He thought back to the feeling of the words flowing through his hands, the actual world receding and the fictional one taking over, and he made another reservation. He had no reason to go to New York, but that room was calling to him, that cold, solitary refuge from life.

Carol-Ann knocked at the door and took a deep breath. She had stayed by him for so long. She stayed with him when he was just a poor wannabe tripping over words in the dictionary. She stayed with him through the initial shock of his first real success. She had stayed with him as his ego shrank and he became scared of the fame. She watched him through a window of his pride as he began to shrink in on himself. She watched him transform from a confident, strong, handsome man to a blithering, self-loathing, vapid pedant.

She watched him decline as her own abilities escalated. She began painting as a hobby but quickly became serious. She had talent—what some people call "the eye." She was brilliant at capturing images. The first painting she sold was of a marble countertop interlaced with a stovetop containing two burners. Both the burners had plastic covering them, as if just purchased. Next to the stovetop was an empty bottle of ketchup, fallen prone with a small, red globule spilling out of the mouth. Carol-Ann called it *Battered Bride Lying on the Altar of Her Missing Husband*. She was the bride.

She sold it in a gallery a week after her husband's first release. He didn't notice she had sold it until a month later.

Carol-Ann's next sale was featured in *Juxtapoze*. It was a candelabra with one burning candle. The wax that slid down transformed into a mustang running, with its mane swimming in the breeze. She called it *The Great Escape*. Once again she was represented in her painting, and once again he didn't notice for a month. This sale came in between *The Correct Ideal for a Failing Marriage* and *The Devastated Sole*, and her husband just didn't seem to hear when she told him.

She got off the phone with her agent, heart beating and eyes tearing. She went to tell him with an unending grin on her face, and she found him in his study, writing. She called to him and said she had just gotten off the phone with her agent. She was going to ask him if he would attend a release party with her because she had just attained clients who were going to pay her to paint—but she never got a chance to. As he sat at his computer, he lifted his right hand with his index finger pointing up, indicating that she should wait. His eyes never left the screen. He brought his hand back down to the keyboard and took a deep breath that said, "Don't ever fucking do that again," and went back to writing.

He started going to hotels to write after that. He wrote every day.

She forgave him, though. She had so much love to give and such a need for belonging, for acceptance. She had never felt ostracism before. Carol-Ann had had a good life so far: she enjoyed a good relationship with her family, and there was never a shortage of money (though to be fair there was never an excess of money either). She'd had two relationships in her life, and they had both ended mutually and quickly and with little hardship. So when she realized she was having trouble with her husband, she ignored the symptoms and internalized her anger and despair. The only time she let her spirit free was in her painting. It was such a cathartic release for her to express her inner longing through the abstract characters she painted, because in her real life, the life in which *he* shared, she repressed her true feelings for fear that he would leave her. She had become complacent and agreeable and had forgotten what life was like before he was in it. So she would dream of leaving and live vicariously through her not-quite-real counterparts.

While Carol-Ann slowly released her inner longings he moved from hotel room to hotel room. He had initially gotten the same hotel room, that room at the Hilton, which had been so productive for him, but it soon wore off. There was something missing since the last time he was there. In his ignorance he couldn't tell that he missed Carol-Ann. She would rub his shoulders when he sat hunched over the screen for too long. She would cook him dinner while he stared at the wall, stretching his mind for what his next chapter would hold. She made love to him even when he had ignored her needs all day long. He just continued to move from room to room and from city to city, gradually getting further and further from Carol-Ann.

To fulfill the void of companionship he started calling sex lines. Sometimes he would just call to talk about his problems or a particular plot problem; sometimes he masturbated to their sensual coos. It never dawned on him to call Carol-Ann, and it never dawned on him that if he did call her, she might think it odd, as if he were only calling because he had a problem. Or maybe it did dawn on him, because he knew that the only time he called her *was* when he had a problem. He justified his jejune behavior by arguing semantics: he wasn't actually penetrating anyone, so he wasn't actually cheating.

He went from hotel to hotel in his search for that lost feeling of creativity, but every hotel room, every mile that separated him from Carol-Ann, seemed to deplete his desire. He was in the midst of writing his fourth novel, the one he had started in the Hilton those few years back, as he awaited her arrival. The book was the chronicle of a woman scorned. She was married to a man who neither paid attention to her nor cared what she did. He loved her dearly, but he didn't know how to show it and instead separated himself with the trappings of his art.

He only wrote what he experienced though, and it was only after years of writing the book that he realized he was writing about his own relationship. In his book the main character was tired of the life she and her husband were living. She almost never saw her husband, and when she did he was cold, distant. She tried to fill her time with crocheting and other meaningless tasks while swallowing her dissatisfaction. The woman (whom he hadn't named yet—even after six hundred manuscript pages) sat at her mirror one day and saw the first vestiges of age, slight crow's feet around her eyes and smile lines surrounding her mouth, and behind her in the room was nothing but emptiness and a small sliver of light shining from the window to the door. She took another look at her aging face and the clearly lighted pathway to the door, and she made a decision: there will be no more lonely nights. It was at this moment, as the scene unfolded on the page, that he finally thought of a name for his heroine. He would name her Angelica, for the nearly spiritual imagery of the light showing her way to freedom and for the celestial patience of his wife Carol-Ann.

When Carol-Ann knocked on the door he realized his mistake. Carol-Ann had seen the sliver of light; she had been shown the door, and she was there to tell him she was leaving. When she knocked, he quickly got up and stood, blocking the door, mute.

"I'm leaving you." She looked at him expectantly. She wanted him to say something. She wanted him to tell her not to leave. She wanted him to tell her he loved her. She wanted him to laugh in her face and take her in his arms and kiss her. He said nothing.

"I'm tired, and I don't like being lonely all the time." He was terrified. His throat was so dry he felt like it was going to crack. He wanted to take her in his arms. He wanted to caress her face and kiss her newly forming tears. He wanted to tell her he would never leave her again. He wanted to tell her he loved her. He said nothing.

"I know you don't care. I don't know why I waited this long. I guess I was just hoping. You're free now." She stood there for a moment and then gave a little frustrated hop. He said nothing.

She turned and walked down the hallway. He raised his hand to her back, imploring her to stay. He wanted to speak, but nothing would come. He thought she would turn back. He thought she would give him one last chance, but Carol-Ann had made up her mind. He had no love for her. He showed that. He said nothing.

He watched her leave the hotel hallway and walk out into the blinding sun. He didn't let his arm fall. His throat croaked, but he didn't say anything.

His arm fell and his mouth closed and he sagged against the doorjamb. He heard a squealing of tires from down the hallway. He had heard the sound many times before, and it always made him cringe. It was one of those sounds that was always followed by a crunch indicative of crumbling plastic and twisted metal. Before he knew what he was doing, he ran down the hallway. He hit the doorway at stride, splashing out into the bright noonday sun. The light blinded him for a moment, time only enough for him to dream he was somewhere else, to dream he was waking from a terrible nightmare in bed next to Carol-Ann. When his eyes focused, he saw her lying on the ground, surrounded by a pool of blood and halfway under a beat-down Ford Taurus.

He had no recollection of it, but he ran to her and cradled her in his arms. Flashes of *The Correct Ideal for a Failing Marriage* ran through his head, and he looked down into her eyes. He said nothing.

"Who are you?" Carol-Ann's brain had been jostled by the impact of the car, damaging her temporal cortex and erasing her ability to remember who he was. He took it to mean that even now, in her death throes, she had not forgiven him. She didn't want him around.

She was just happy to have someone hold her, finally getting the intimate contact her relationship had lost.

As he lay there with her body, as she slowly slipped away, he thought back to the last thing he wrote:

The most amazing thing about her is her ability to see past my bad habits. She can ignore my imperfections and treat me like a man, while I deal with what I have to. It wasn't until she came to the door that I realized how much I loved her. She came to tell me she was leaving, and I loved her more than I ever had. Ever. In that moment I knew all I had to do was tell her those few words and everything would be okay. Everything would be as it should. All I had to do was say those three words.

"I love you, Carol-Ann."

Dark Secret

Dan flips through the videos while the computer projects its blue-white light through the dark room. He's been at it for hours, but then again that's the beauty of the job. He can do it anytime, anywhere, and best of all he can work at home.

Dan has been a moderator for YouTube for about a year. His entire job entails surfing videos, and then when he finds one with unsatisfactory content (that's the word his boss uses, *unsatisfactory*, with a pedantic little lisp) he deletes it and blocks the user from posting again. Some might think this a boring job, a pointless job, but Dan loves it.

He decides tonight he'll concentrate on porn, mostly because he's feeling horny himself, but also because he hasn't surfed the "sexuality videos" for at least three days. He spent that time on animal abuse and violence.

He types "asian sex" into the search bar and cracks his knuckles by weaving his fingers together and dramatically swooping them out toward the computer. He holds back a little smile and then lets his right hand rest on the mouse, slowly scrolling down through his options.

There are a surprising amount of trick videos, like "two lesbians having SeX!" and "Penetration! Asian SLut!" Dan hates these tricky ones. He always clicks on them, ready to cancel the account, but when the video comes up, six times out of eight it's some douche bag who has too much time on his hands with a note saying "pervert!" and pictures of little animals and babies. To Dan these are a waste of time. Why would someone go through all that effort just to berate another?

This time, though, it's different. He logs on, and the first video that comes up says, "Sexy asian girl dancing." Most times Dan passes by things like this because almost invariably it'll only be a girl dancing on a webcam feed— nothing you couldn't see out on the street. But there are occasions when he finds an older man forcing a preteen to do a striptease. He forwards those on to the police and bans the user from the site. But, this time it's different.

He clicks on the link, and she comes on. It *is* as he expects, probably a self-taping on a webcam, a co-ed doing a booty dance. He feels a brief second of sorrow for the girl, trying to imagine what happens to girls like this in an Asian culture. *Don't women get disowned for this kind of thing?* he thinks. He shakes his head and clicks the play button.

It starts with her face covering the screen, giving him a distinct and startling view of her expressionless physiognomy. An intermittent guitar riff blares over his speakers. She slowly backs up and briefly gives Dan a view of a few hastily scrawled words written in a red liquid on the blue wall behind her—"Dead now," he thinks they say—and he immediately feels cold. *What if it's in blood?* he thinks. But before he can tell, she deftly dances in front of it. The music continues: "Make up your mind/Decide to walk with me/Around the lake tonight ..."

She's wearing a little, tight, white T-shirt, and underneath she's wearing a pink bra. Her bottoms are a white pair of short shorts, giving full view of her great legs. She begins to slowly wave her hips back and forth, out of tempo with the music, while looking directly at the camera. Her eyes are intense, and he finds he can't tear his from hers, those deep hazel spotlights.

"... I'll not be a gentleman/Behind the boathouse/I'll show you my dark secret ..."

Suddenly, she snaps her head to the side, breaking eye contact, and slowly weaves her body, as smooth as a snake, until her back is facing the camera. Dan's eyes are drawn to her ass, where written on her little white short shorts in red block lettering is the word *lifeguard*. As if to emphasize this, she brings both arms up, sensuously dancing and weaving them in the air, and then brings them down and points both her index fingers at the word, framing it. *She actually points at it*, Dan thinks. When she turns back again, her face looks intent, and her hazel eyes burn into the camera.

"... Don't be afraid/I don't mean to scare you/So help me, Jesus ..."

She crosses her arms and grabs the bottom of her shirt beginning to pull it up, and then turns again. Dan can see little bits of the scrawling behind her as she sways her body, and he is sure he was right. It says "Dead now" in red, dripping letters.

My God, is *that blood?* he wonders.

"… I can promise you/You'll stay as beautiful …"

Her back's to him again, and she takes the shirt off, her long brown hair cascading across her deltoids. She then turns again and looks deep into the camera. She looks almost nervous.

On her stomach there's an arrow pointing at her left breast. It's a decal that almost looks like wood. When he follows the arrow, he sees something that further disturbs him. The pink bra is actually a white bra, stained red. The left side is darker than the right.

"… with dark hair/And soft skin/Forever …"

Unnerved he looks back down to the time bar, hoping the video is nearing completion, but it isn't moving. The ball tracker is still on the left, and the counter says 0:00. He looks back at the screen, and she's staring at him, barely moving, with an imploring stare.

She turns again, reaching up for her bra with both hands and begins to unhook it. "… Forever …" Then the screen goes black. Dan sits back and takes a deep breath, realizing how close he was to the screen.

"Holy shit," he says. He flags the video but doesn't erase it.

There are dreams that you can tell are dreams—where reality is thin, and you can feel it. Dan's having one of those now of his little Asian girl.

She's doing the same dance, but this time he's in the room with her. It's the same room as in the video with few exceptions. "Dead now" is gone from the wall behind her, and he's sitting in a chair where the camera must have been.

She backs away from him and takes position a few feet away. Her movements have a jerky, halting progress as if she's a projection. She does her little shimmy, the same as before, but there are little details Dan notices that he didn't notice watching the MPEG. When she points at *lifeguard*, written on her shorts, she flexes a bit. Not much but enough for Dan to see veins straining in her wrists. She spends longer than he remembers, jerking her fingers and flexing even more, accentuating the word. It's like she's saying, "Pay attention."

Then she turns and takes off her shirt while mouthing words to him as the cotton crests over her mouth: "Find me."

Of course it could have been a multitude of other phrases, but he's sure she sneers, a tiny raise of her upper lip, as she spits out the letter f with a breathy "fuh."

Desire for her invades his mind, overtaking his soul. He wants to stand and put his arms around her, wants to kiss her. But in that special reality dreams create, he's stuck to his chair, no matter how much effort he puts into it.

He looks up at her and sees her nodding at him, ever so slightly, but never taking her eyes from his. She moves forward and puts her arms out, beckoning him to embrace her, and blood starts to pour from her left C cup, pouring over the seam where fabric meets flesh and staining the white bra a deeper shade of burgundy. Then she mouths it again: "Find me."

Dan wakes the next morning both disturbed and inquisitive. He knows it was only a creepy dream, but he can't shake how *real* it felt, as if he could watch the video and all the changes from the dream would be there. He just *has* to watch the video. Just one more time.

Dan gets up from his sweat-soaked bed and lights a cigarette on the way to the computer. "Well, lets just see here," he croaks through a lung full of smoke.

He turns his computer on, producing a bright blue light that shines into the room, illuminating the smoke and its seductive wave as it sways to the ceiling. It makes him think of her.

He shakes his head and goes back to the computer, clicking the link to bring her up. He has a brief reminiscence of her hair and the way it draped over her shoulders. He thinks in the dream, it may have touched his chest when she began to dance, but then again it was only a dream, a phantom of sensation.

The phone rings with an alarmed, repetitive bleating, and he looks back at it in disdain, angry at its audacity, intruding on his viewing. But then he hears the soft hitching electric guitar coming from the computer, and he whips his head around to see the show begin. He knows it's probably his boss on the phone trying to document his progress through the "unsatisfactory" videos. He knows he could be in trouble if he doesn't answer, but he just has to see the video. Just one more time.

Everything from the dream is there. She pumps her hands twice at *lifeguard*. She says "Find me" just before the shirt covers her face. She *does* bleed a bit at the end, and those arms *do* rise.

"She's telling me something," Dan says through the smoke as the phone blares in the background. "She's in trouble."

He gets up long enough to grab a pad and a pen, and then he sits down and scrawls an inventory of every detail he thinks could be important.

1. Find me
2. Lifeguard
3. Dead now
4. Arrow to bloody bra

Dan puts his hand to his left breast, a reflex as he recalls the image of her bloody breast, and recognition lights his face. It was something he did every day as a child in elementary school. He put his right hand over his heart. Pledging.

He clicks the play button, and the dead lifeguard comes back on the screen, swaying and shaking. He peers into the video and tries to find more clues; finding none, he peruses his list again. She's a lifeguard, so she must be by a body of water. A lake? A pool? A beach? But then lifeguards are usually only out during peak hours. Too many people. Then the song lyrics strike him. "… Decide to walk with me/Around the lake tonight …" She *was* telling him something!

While he's contemplating, Pocket, his tabby cat, saunters into the room. He's made it a rule that the cat stay out of the room whenever he's working because, for some reason known only to troublemaking cats, she loves to bat the power cord until it's pulled from the wall. It isn't a big deal, really, but when he's lost in his videos it infuriates him.

Dan clicks the play button again, desperately searching for any hint that might tell him something. When she moves back and "dead now" becomes visible, he finds what he's looking for.

He's not sure why he didn't notice it before, but those two cryptic words are actually written *on* something, not directly on the wall. They're written on a map. A map with a lake on it. A map of his town.

He pauses the video, grasps his flat-screen monitor with both hands and leans in, straining his eyes in an attempt to decipher where she could possibly be, when he feels the familiar brush of fur against his leg. His eyes widen, and he reaches under the table, grabbing for Pocket. But he's too late. The cat bats the cord, and a small popping sound comes from the computer as it goes blank. Pocket coos as she runs from the room.

Dan quickly plugs the computer back in and presses the power button. The computer's fan issues a high whine, and the monitor flickers with a blue flash and then a faded black glow. He thinks for a moment he can see her body shake on the screen, a shadow in the dark, but then his wallpaper pops up. He quickly opens the video files on his desktop, searching for his China girl. But she's not there.

Dan clicks around in anger. "What the fuck!" he screams at the monitor, waving his left hand in disgust. "Come on, you stupid piece of shit!" He slams his fist on the desk in anger and sits back. "Where the hell...?"

He takes a deep breath and relaxes. So what? So what if when Pocket knocked out the cord the video got erased? Maybe he didn't even save it on his desktop in the first place. There's still that beautiful network that serves billions. She would still be on the Internet!

He navigates to YouTube and types in his password, which redirects him into his moderator screen. The video should be in the recently viewed column. Even the memory of it would be there, a name at least. But when he searches, he finds nothing. The username of the person who downloaded it isn't even there. The last video it says he's watched is of a cat getting hit by a car.

Scared, Dan stands. He gazes into the screen, perplexed and more than just a little bit worried. Was he delusional? Could none of this have happened? That dance though. Sexual and sensual, torrid and disturbing. He couldn't forget her hazel eyes. The way her breath felt ...

"Wait ..." He snaps out of his reverie. *Did I imagine her breath?* It was a video. He knows none of it was real, yet he can feel the memory of her breath on his face, smell the sweet staleness as she leaned down and began her dance, with her breasts sagging ever so slightly and her hair brushing his chest.

He stops thinking and blinks twice. Hard.

"You need to get to sleep, that's all," he says and is scared by his own voice. He realizes just how quiet it's been in the room, and he feels the constant presence of eyes in every corner. He looks about quickly, securing all shadows, and promptly turns on the lights. He flips the TV on, thankful for the resounding echo it creates in the small room and lets its soft waves lull him into complacency. Then he dreams.

Here she is again, swaying in front of him, although this time she looks wet. Her white shirt is clinging even more tightly to her youthful stomach, and he can easily see the bloodstained bra beneath. She moves in stop-action jerks and mouths over and over again. "Find me. Find me. Find me."

She looks deep into his eyes, and he's lost in her sea of hazel. Mystified. Compelled. He sits up and shudders as the absolute coldness of the room embraces him. Then he remembers something. Something from his childhood. It's reflected in her eyes. He finds himself putting his hand over his heart as he did so many times as a child, recalling the Pledge of Allegiance ... and that other time he used to put his hand over his heart, when his uncle took him fishing out on Lake Meneloua. He remembers promising he would never tell—cross his heart—as they

would pass a big red arrow pointing at an angle up to
the heart of the lake. He remembers his uncle saying,
"This place is dangerous. Never come alone and always let
someone know you're here. No one really comes around
here anymore." He remembers the boathouse where they
stored their supplies. He remembers the sign on the door
to the shed. It said, "Danger, heavy pollution" in hazel
letters. He knows where she is. He has to find her.

The red arrow is still as shiny and glossy as he remembers
it being, almost as if the paint were still wet. The arrow
zips by as his Tercel glides down the road, and Dan fidgets
in anticipation as the lake gets ever closer.

He thinks back to his time on the lake with his uncle,
the depth and murkiness of the water like a primordial
soup, thick and teeming with small, unfamiliar creatures.
He remembers feeling both distinctly disgusted and
slightly exhilarated when his uncle caught a big fish and
rocked the boat, nearly sending little Danny into the lake.
To sink in there is to never be found again.

He drives past the boathouse where they kept their
fishing equipment, and he smiles despite his anxiousness.
*If old Uncle Walt weren't dead, he'd probably love to be here
with me,* he thinks.

There's a beach on the lake about a quarter mile more
down the road. It's a deserted beach now, but twenty
years ago it was bustling with activity. Children played

in the soft surf as their parents lounged and tanned by the afternoon sun while a lone lifeguard watched over the lake waters from a sole tower. The lake had since been deemed too polluted to be a place of recreation, so gradually over the years people stopped going. This is where he's headed—to find the lifeguard.

He's able to get most of the way to the beach before the road becomes too overgrown and he has to ditch the Tercel. He's taken aback at the beauty of the place. There are rays of sunlight beaming through the treetops and casting an almost holy glow about the overgrown road, lending the shade an almost picturesque totality. He can feel the onslaught of a sneeze coming as the pollen from the unmolested flowering buds slowly falls on him. He lets it go with remarkable furiousness, making his head feel like it's going to explode.

He is covering his nose and mouth with his hand, trying to block pollen from entering his system, when he comes to the clearing of the beach. The white sand goes on for a hundred yards and is cradled by the tree line, making it feel like a secluded oasis. The lone lifeguard tower stands halfway through the white dunes and is painted red just like the arrow on the road.

Another sneeze rocks Dan, and he groans as he stands on the precipice of the beach. Terrified to move forward, he hopes he'll find the girl, but he also feels deep instilled dread of what he might find. He feels his knees shaking and tells himself it's from sneezing, but he knows it's his fear. He can smell it—dank and bitter.

He takes a shaky step forward, and his shoe sinks into the warm white sand. He imagines for a moment he's on a deserted island, trying to dissolve his fear, but then he looks out onto the lake and sees the familiar bowling-pin-shaped buoy floating in the water. He used to try to cast his reel at the buoy, practicing his fly-fishing while his uncle looked on, smirking.

The memory brings him back to reality, and he closes his eyes as he takes a deep breath. He sneezes again, bellowing echoes around the small enclosure.

Shaking his head, he moves forward and takes out his phone. If there is even a chance of seeing a dead body, he wants to be on the phone with the police immediately. He's not sure how he's going to explain it, but it's better than being out here alone with a corpse.

He's halfway down the beach when he sees her. She's lying face down in the wet sand, half in the water and half out. He can see her hair splayed about her head in a halo and flashes back to her dance. That beautiful hair brushing up against his chest. He immediately knows it's her. He dials 911 on his phone and takes a few steps forward, trying, against his better judgment, to get a better look at her.

He gives the dispatcher the location and explains that he found a body on a walk. He gives his name and phone number and hangs up, despite the dispatcher's protests, and looks back at the body.

She's wearing corduroy pants and a jean jacket. Dan almost snickers despite himself, imagining her walking around in some nineties movie like *Singles* but is brought back home when he gets a whiff of her smell.

She must've been out here for days. The smell attacks his nose, like a forgotten steak left on a counter. He can hear a soft buzzing sound and knows it's flies convening for their feast. Her legs are lost in the soft surf, and he can only imagine what two days in contaminated water would do to a decomposing body, bloated and white, slowly sloughing flesh off the bone.

Dan reaches down and taps the back of her head, a playful tap, as if he's tagging her IT. He's not sure why he does it; he knows she's dead, yet he has a morbid curiosity to feel what it would be like to touch her. It's almost as if he's testing himself for what he has to do next.

He's found her, but he doesn't feel she's done with him quite yet. He's not sure what it is, but he gets the nagging suspicion he's being watched, as if her ghost followed him here, out through the computer screen and into this world. He whirls around in an effort to see her, to figure out where she's hiding, but there's nothing—just him and the shining white sand with the lone red lifeguard aerie of safety.

He turns back to her and grabs one shoulder without really thinking about it, turning her to her back. He's surprised at how stiff she is, rigor mortis freezing her body into shape.

The first thing he sees is her eyes. He's surprised to see that they're brown and only shells, merely reflectors in the afternoon sun. They show no resplendence of their own. Then he sees her chest. There is a thin hole with something shiny protruding through the red-stained blouse she wears. When he leans in closer, he finds it's a butter knife. Damn near buried to the hilt. Right through her heart.

Dan covers his mouth in disgust and feels another sneeze coming on. He can feel bile rising in his throat, and he turns away from her lifeless eyes.

The sneeze builds in his nose, and he fights it, fearing that if he does sneeze, vomit will come with it. So he stands there for a moment pinching the arch of his nose until the sneeze subsides, and then he slowly turns back to the girl.

Her body undulates with the soft surf, and he stands transfixed until he hears something from the woods behind him, a powerful sneeze and a rattle of leaves.

Dan whips around, peering out into the woods, and there by the clearing is a small Asian man pointing a gun at him.

"Whoa, man! Whoa!" Dan wants to say something evocative and powerful, but the sight of the gun takes the breath from his lungs.

"What you do here?" the man shouts with an almost rodent-like squeal. "You not supposed to be here!"

"I'm sorry! I know, I'm sorry! Please!" Terror grips Dan, and he looks down at the dead girl next to him. At that moment he's sure he's not going to get out of here alive.

"No sorry! No please! That what she said! Fucking cheating slut!" He points to the corpse on the ground for the briefest of moments with the gun, and Dan's heart flutters with hope.

"I'll just go. I didn't mean anything ..." He tries to make his voice soothing, but he hears instead that it's slow and hitching like he's going to start crying.

"*No. Go*!" The man actually takes a deep breath in between the two words and screams "*Go*!" like a child throwing a temper tantrum.

The gun trains back on Dan.

"Okay, okay, I'm sorry." Dan takes a step back and feels the cool polluted waters of Lake Meneloua surrounding his feet. For the first time the shit-like smell of the lake hits his nostrils as it mixes with the rot of the lifeguard's corpse, gagging him.

The man moves a few steps toward him, and Dan notices he's filthy. He has leaves in his hair, his clothes are covered with a fine layer of pollen, and his shins are slicked with wet sand and mud. His outfit matches hers. "You lay down with her! You fuck her?"

The question catches Dan off guard.

"No!" is all he can say, as he walks knee-deep into the poisonous waters of Lake Meneloua. He feels the water rush around him, and he swallows bile as the surrounding water bubbles with pollution.

"You fuck her! I know you do!" The man takes a few steps forward, bobbing the gun at Dan. Dan inches backward, further into the water. He thinks back to a time in his childhood when he used to swim here and remembers a shelf in the sand just a few feet away from the shore. Maybe five. After that shelf, the lake floor drops. If he can get to that point maybe he can swim away.

"Don't you move, you—" The man stops in mid-sentence and sneers, shaking his head rapidly, and then sneezes fiercely, snapping his head and rocking his body.

Great. Sneeze your brains out, you crazy bastard! Dan thinks. He inches himself further backward into the water. He feels something slide along his leg in the shallow surf and retches, projecting vomit into the water. While he's doubled over, he looks at the girl, stares into her brown eyes, and swears he can see concern in her death mask.

The man recovers and moves forward a few steps, cocking the gun, apparently done with cordialities.

"Wait! When I saw the body I called the police! You should leave!" Dan yells when he hears the hammer click back.

The man pauses for a moment, looking confused, and then sneezes again. Dan steps a few inches back into the water, praying the ledge isn't too far away. The man raises the gun to him again, contorts his face, and screams, "You lie!" He sneezes one more time.

Dan takes the opportunity and jumps backward, using every bit of agility he has, and lands on his back in the water. He can feel the ledge with his hand, but he didn't quite make it.

"You fuck!" the man yells. He shoots the gun three times in rapid succession. The first shot buries in the water to the left of Dan, the second in front of him, and the third to the right.

Without thinking, Dan throws himself back again and slides over the ridge, sinking into the putrid lake. He hears more gunfire—three more shots, he thinks—and swims away from the edge. His skin burns as he strokes through the murky water, and he imagines the smell permeating his skin.

Finally Dan can go no further and, preferring to be shot rather than swallow the lake water, he surfaces, disappointed to realize he's only gone twenty feet. The man is at the edge of the lake, actually standing over the girl, and he raises the gun, aiming for Dan's face. Dan takes a deep breath of the rancid air and goes below again, hearing the report of gunfire three more times. *That was nine wasn't it?* Dan thinks. Desperately he swims toward shore, hoping the man will have to reload before he can fire again.

Dan gets to the shelf in the water and springs up, pushing with all his might from the bottom of the lake and resurfacing directly in front of the man. Everything smells so bad that Dan imagines little cartoon wisps of stink rising off him.

The man jumps back and sneezes in surprise as Dan jumps on him. The man screams as Dan grapples him, though Dan imagines it's more from the stink than from anything else.

It's a short match. Dan wrenches the gun away from the man and sits on his chest, giving him one great punch to the nose, relishing the snap he feels beneath his knuckles. He's about to do it again when he hears someone shout at them.

"Freeze!"

They both look up and see two policemen with their weapons drawn and trained on the two of them. Dan sits back and gradually stands with his arms raised. Ever so slowly, he steps away from the man on the ground.

"You, on the ground! Stand with your arms raised!" the alpha cop says, while the other slowly circles around to the right.

The man on the ground sneezes again and then looks at the girl lying next to him. Suddenly the air seems to get thicker, and everything slows down. The man on the ground lunges for the gun, and Dan can hear the alpha cop yelling something; but he's so amazed at this little man's audacity that he doesn't understand. Dan falls to the ground as the little man pops up and points the gun. Dan can hears three distinct resounding explosions in the little oasis, and then hears a thud as the man hits the ground next to him. Dan looks at him, into his brown eyes, and watches as the light fades.

As he stares into the dead man's eyes, Dan thinks back to what his uncle said all those years ago: *This is a dangerous place. Never come alone and always let someone know you're here.* "Thanks for looking after me, Uncle Walt," Dan says under his breath.

The cops walk over to Dan, still training their guns at him. "Who are you, and why're you here?"

Dan turns over and looks up at the policeman. He puts his hands above his head and says, "My name's Dan. I just thought I'd go out for some fishing."

Purgatory

P eople speak of redemption as if it were reserved for good deeds, as if the only way to be redeemed is to save someone or sacrifice yourself. Clark, however, knew of another way to reach heaven, through a place in between, a place where redemption is not achieved by apologizing for transgressions—but by suffering for them.

Clark approached the house and thought of old clichés: the house looked like a face. The upper windows looked like eyes, a smaller grill a nose, and the large double doors a gaping mouth. He felt as though he was in an old film like *The Amityville Horror*; dread filled him as he walked to the house. Clark had to go in, though. It was his job.

Clark was a real estate agent who had gotten flaked on by his renovation crew. They never showed, and they never called; they wouldn't even answer when he called them.

"Some renovation company," Clark muttered as he

clutched his car keys tightly in his hand, wrapping the key ring around his middle finger. He felt loathing seep into his bones as he crept toward the house. Toward the face.

It was a pristine location; the woods were back just enough to give this Victorian a foundation, and they fit snugly around the sides. A beautiful brick pathway led from the back door to the guesthouse a few hundred feet away. Arched trees lined the pathway, casting shadows over the delicately laid stones of the path. It was like something out of a fairy tale. The lawn and the pathway down to the guesthouse had been groomed with precision. It seemed as if the vegetation only grew to a certain point and then stopped rendering pruning useless. The property was supposed to be dilapidated and unsellable, vacant for twenty years, but it looked as if someone had been there very recently.

Clark looked back at the road, back to his car which was perched so nicely on the cut-stone driveway, then to the gazebo in the front yard, and finally to the gothic statues displayed so artfully in the yard. He just had to wonder, *What's wrong with this house?* Why had the other company not sold it?

He walked to the front door and twisted the handle. He expected to hear creaking joints, a weathered metal-on-metal sound indicative of old hinges, but no sound came. The door slowly and smoothly swung open, revealing how lazy the other real estate company had been.

They had recommended a renovation crew, and this was obviously the reason why: the house was a shambles. There was graffiti covering the interior of the foyer; the floorboards were rotten, the walls moldy, and everything just looked old. Wooden furniture was devastated by termites; white cloths were stained yellow by sunlight; dust and time covered what was not already falling apart. Clark gaped in horror at the decrepit state of the place.

He slowly shook his head in disgust. Then, as he turned to swing the door shut, he heard a guttural growl from outside.

Clark froze, imagining the animals who could wander in from the forest in the night—yet another reason why this place could've lain dormant for so long.

Clark took a hesitant step toward the doorway, craning his neck in an effort to see where the noise came from, all the while holding a firm grip on the front door so he could swing it shut in the face of anything that might come loping after him. He peered out but saw nothing. Then the growl came again, this time sounding more urgent and much closer.

Clark slammed the door shut, picked up a nearby chair, and propped it against the door handle. He backed through the room and looked around to see if he could find a window that would give him a look at the beast as it made its way through the foliage. But there was no beast. It was a man running through the woods. Clark felt a wave of terror wash over him as he whipped around, trying to find a weapon. As he did so a figure passed through the hallway into another room.

"Hello?" Clark softly called out, his throat closing. "This is private property. You can't be here." It wasn't an order.

Clark took a step forward, looking around the foyer and still trying to find some kind of weapon. He was in the middle of a robbery! He was sure of it! He needed to hide and hope that they hadn't seen him.

And he still needed a weapon. He looked around the room, and at first saw nothing. He reached up to lean on the mantle to rest and come up with a plan, but when he did so he felt something in his hand poke him. His car keys. He had forgotten they were there. He slipped them off, put them on the mantle, and rubbed his hand. Then, from the corner of his eye, a bright glint of light caught his attention. He turned to look and saw the only thing that might pass for a weapon in the room.

He picked up an umbrella; a slight smile threatened his face but then went away. The umbrella did have a sharp metal tip, but it wasn't a suitable weapon, and Clark knew it.

He pointed it like a talisman to the spot where the figure had walked and crept toward the far wall while keeping an eye on the empty corridor.

When he got to the wall, someone started pounding on the front door, roaring in rage and frustration. Clark nearly screamed himself but instead ran straight for the hallway that the figure had come from, hoping he wouldn't come back.

The pounding on the front door stopped just as Clark made it to the bathroom.

He could *hear* his heart pounding. He shut his eyes and leaned back against the door, wishing whomever it was would go away. For several minutes, eyes closed and breathing lightly, he tried to keep a hold on his fear. He focused, listening intently for any movement outside the door, but he heard nothing.

He slowly opened his eyes and took a look around the bathroom. It was a normal, spartan bathroom. The walls were painted in a pale seventies yellow, and flower wallpaper adorned the lower half. There was a small sink in front of him and a toilet next to that, with a standing shower in the corner—and a small elevated window behind him.

Clark stood on his tiptoes, excited, thinking he might have finally found his way out. He flung the window open, threw out the umbrella, and pulled himself up to the opening. While squeezing through the window he froze in horror.

Outside in the woods he saw *another* man walking through the shadows. He stopped and looked over at Clark. Clark tried to scream but instead dropped back down to the floor of the bathroom, whimpering. He felt isolated, surrounded. Clark could feel a cold sweat breaking out on his brow. *Jesus! Everything was so normal a minute ago!* he thought. He looked around the room and made his decision. He would make a break for it. He slowly stood up, trying to stay away from the window, and went to the sink. He looked at himself in the mirror and was shocked. He looked like he hadn't slept in days; his eyes were red and watery, and his skin was pale.

He looked down to turn on the water but stopped when he saw something moving in the drain. He bent down, edging closer, trying to determine what it was, and hoping it wasn't a rat. It wasn't. The drain held a human eye. It moved as if it were looking about the room, and then it looked straight at him. Laughter echoed, resonating in the pipes of the drain. The laughter was steeped in madness.

Clark lunged backward and landed on his ass. He gazed about the room, hoping for an exit to appear so he could leave this nightmare, but the only option was the bathroom door. He got up and slowly turned the handle, inching the door open. He looked down at the empty hallway and let out a small breath. He was trying to be as quiet as he could; there was no sense in alerting anyone who might be in the house.

Clark took a small step forward into the hallway, dreading having to leave his sanctuary, but he knew he couldn't just wait for someone to root him out.

On his second step, the doorknob to the front door turned. Clark froze. They were everywhere. He had to make a break for it. Clark quickly walked down the hallway, keeping his head down and moving as silently as possible. He passed the room without any problem, and he felt relieved. Since the front door wasn't an option any longer, he needed a back door or another window—except there was someone in the woods and at least one more person in the house. With another at the front door.

The hallway went another ten feet past the living

room archway, with a view of the front door, and turned to the right, leading deeper into the house. There were no windows in the hallway.

Clark walked forward, turned the corner, and saw a kitchen at the end of the hallway with something he desperately needed: a window.

Clark made his way slowly, same as before, to the window. Excited, he swung a leg over the windowsill but paused when the door directly to his right opened. The kitchen he was in was bare and clean with a thin door that led to the backyard. The door opened in, and he could see a figure coming in through a blinded window. The man from outside.

Clark threw himself out the window as he heard someone walking to the kitchen from the hallway behind him. He hit the ground outside and ran for the guesthouse in the back. His heart was pounding, and his lungs burned from the cold air; but he thought if he could get away and hide, he could be safe—and what better place than the guesthouse? There wouldn't be anything valuable in there for the thieves to steal. It would be empty. It had to be.

He got to the guesthouse and opened the door. Then a terrible truth hit him. The guesthouse *was* empty, but so was the house. These weren't thieves; they weren't there to steal from the house. There was nothing in the house. They were there for something else. He had parked his car out front. They knew he was there. They would know he was out in the guesthouse now and come after him. Again, he needed a weapon.

He let go of the door handle and went stalking into the woods, hunched over. He was trying to be as quiet as possible, but he could hear someone back at the guesthouse. He turned to look toward the house and saw someone climbing out of the bathroom window, looking at him. Clark only saw the person for a moment, but he could tell the person had spotted him because he ducked down as soon as Clark looked over.

These people are sadists, he thought. They knew he was there, but they weren't doing anything to him. They were playing with him. He had to get to his car and get out of there.

He took a few running steps and heard a car door shut. *His* car door. *You've gotta be kidding me!* Clark thought, sprinting toward the car and growling in anger. He heard the front door of the house slam shut, and he stopped growling. Clark wasn't fooled. He knew they were probably trying to set a trap for him; he just didn't know what it was. He reached into his pocket to get the keys and froze. The keys weren't in his pocket! He looked up at the house, and the house looked back at him. The keys were on the mantle.

Clark needed a plan—and fast. He needed to find a way in so he could get those keys back; he didn't have any chance out in the woods.

He circled the house on the opposite side of where he had last seen the sadists, hoping there wouldn't be any more than he had already encountered. He thought about the umbrella lying underneath the bathroom window but knew they would be waiting there for him. Why were they waiting? *Why don't they come and get me?* He had to do something they wouldn't be expecting. He decided to walk around to the kitchen and go in the back entrance.

When he reached the back corner of the house, he took a deep breath in an effort to bolster his courage and then made a crouched run for the door. When he got there he took another deep breath, mustering every ounce of his strength and tenacity. Then he opened the door. The kitchen was empty. Clark nearly cried with relief. He slowly closed the kitchen door and got on his hands and knees. His breath was hitching in fear.

He had only traveled five feet when a loud bang echoed in the room, almost as if someone had hit the house. Clark panicked and opened the nearest door to hide from the assailant. It took him a good few seconds to look around and see where he was. He found himself standing at the top of a staircase leading down into the basement, dark and gothic, with lit torches against the walls, just barely illuminating the staircase.

He felt his mind slip a bit when he laid eyes on the staircase. This wasn't part of the house description. The listing made no mention of a dark pathway leading to a gothic dungeon. But what was even stranger was the figure walking down the staircase. When he looked closer, his heart jumped. Something wasn't right.

The figure was *him.*

He watched as his doppelganger reached the bottom of the staircase and stepped onto the basement landing.

Before he realized what he was doing, Clark walked down after his doppelganger to the basement. It was dingy and poorly lit. Torchlight flickered in the room, licking the walls with their dim luminescence. His doppelganger walked through the wavering light and into the shadows. It crossed the room, reached a ladder at the far side, and slowly started ascending. Clark had almost reached the landing when he heard the door open behind him.

His brain nearly broke trying to come up with a reason for what was happening. Could this be it? Could this be the end of his fabulous career in swindling people into houses they couldn't afford? He let his legs take him to the ladder, and his eyes closed in terror. Whatever was going on, it had to almost be over. He reached out and felt the harsh reality of the ladder, the coarse, splintered wood, and started climbing.

When he looked up, he found he was headed into a crawl space. There was a cylinder of light coming from a pipe above him. *Purgatory is retribution,* Clark thought as he placed his eye to the pipe only to see himself in the house's bathroom looking back down at him through the sink, *and repetition is hell.*

Oh, how he laughed.

The Hypothesis

"When you look up into the sky, what do you see?" Hercule Lambert asked the panel as he gestured to the screen displaying the famous Eagle Nebula. "I see opportunity. I see beauty. I see mystery. Ladies and gentlemen, many of you may have heard of the meteorite fragments that hit earth recently. They show a consistency which we have never seen from space, forming three layers of remarkable material." Hercule pressed the button on the clicker clutched in his hand, and the image on the screen changed to a picture of a crushed ball of metal.

"This, my fellow sentient beings, is the first incontrovertible proof that we are not alone in this universe … or at least … in this multiverse. What you see on the screen is a ball of aluminum alloy. For those of you who don't know, aluminum allow is not a natural substance. It has to be created in a lab by an intelligent creature who understands basic chemistry."

Hercule paused for a moment trying to rein in his excitement as the crowd began to murmur. He slowly let a smile cross his face, knowing he'd captured his audience, and continued on.

"Shocking, isn't it? Now I know many of you are thinking I'm pulling your leg or that the alloy must have been jettisoned from some satellite we already had floating out in space. Well, I can tell you for a certainty, it does not belong to the United States, and I can also assure you it doesn't hail from any other country on Earth; but we'll get to that in a moment."

He clicked the button once again, and the image changed to a twisted cage of metal with bubbles scattered throughout.

"What you are now seeing is our mystery comet with the top layer of aluminum alloy peeled back to reveal a most unusual skeleton. It looks like this skeleton was crushed along with the aluminum that served as the comet's skin. This skeleton is made of a new material scientists are just now trying to incorporate into space shuttle production. It's amorphous steel that is ostensibly a bulk metallic glass. Think of it as a space-age pyrite. It has amazing magnetic, radiation, and thermal durability. This material is just in its infancy; the theorem was originally published in 2004 but has never been fully developed.

"While you ruminate on the possibilities of what that means, turn your attention to the pustules on this remarkable material." Hercule clicked again, and a close-up of the bubbled metal appeared on the screen.

"These pustules are filled with a familiar by-product of the Earth's unique atmosphere: hydrogen dioxide. Or in layman's terms … water. At this point we don't know how water formed in these pustules. There is speculation that it's merely condensation from its vast journey, and there is also a hypothesis that it was created that way to further its thermal qualities. In either case the research for that particular answer is still ongoing."

The room exploded into questions and conversations, which echoed through the room as reporters pressed for information. Hercule mentally patted himself on the back, knowing he inspired this pandemonium, but before he could truly enjoy it, a man from the back shouted out, "You said you had proof this didn't come from another country! How can you prove that?" Panic weaved delicately in his voice.

Hercule smiled and raised his hands, indicating that the audience should quiet down.

"If another Cold War is what you're worried about, there is nothing to fear. I could never be more certain: this meteor did not come from another country." He looked about the room, letting the forcefulness and power of his statement sink in. "You see, once we uncovered this pustule-laden glass steel, we decided to take an extra precaution. We asked ourselves, where could this have come from? Deciding that the possibilities were too endless, we set the sphere into a vacuum chamber for extra precaution. It was during this process that we found the most interesting component of the comet."

Hercule paused for dramatic effect with his hands

crossed in front of his belt, smiling at the collective eagerly waiting his response. When he was satisfied with the drama created, he turned toward the screen, lifted the hand with which he held the clicker, and theatrically switched to the next image. Inwardly Hercule knew it would be anticlimactic, but he couldn't hold in his glee. He was about to uncover the means to understanding the universe, the means to unravel the fabric of space-time.

"What is it?" a confused journalist responded.

"This little ball you see is a container. The contents are a most remarkable revelation." He took two steps forward, covering the light from the projector and fully facing his captive audience. "We calculated the trajectory of the comet and found it came from just outside of M51, otherwise known as the Whirlpool Galaxy. Using these calculations we focused the Chandra X-ray Observatory on the area and found yet another astonishing revelation. Chandra was able to take pictures of a phenomenon previously only hypothesized ... a naked singularity. This enigma is basically a black hole with no event horizon, just an exposed singularity.

"A black hole is created when a massive star uses all its radioactive gasses and collapses on itself. This creates an incredible gravitational field, called an event horizon, surrounding a pinpoint of matter with infinite density, called a singularity. A naked singularity is that pinpoint of incredible density but without the event horizon.

"What makes these monsters of the universe so terrifying is that, if you approach a black hole, the intense gravitational pull will slowly pull your molecules apart like taffy, stretching them beyond their molecular bond capacities. Then once you reach the singularity the density of matter will crush your molecules in through a passageway no larger than a pinhole. One prevailing theory is that a black hole is a portal; thus the singularity is the doorway. If that description is too esoteric, imagine while passing through the singularity, every molecule in your body being pulled apart and then reapplied at the speed of light—and oh, by the way, they won't necessarily be put back in the same molecular structure on the other side. Have you ever seen *The Fly*?"

Hercule smiled at his own cleverness as the journalists gasped and made retching sounds.

"But you still haven't explained why it can't be from another country!" a pugnacious journalist offered.

"We are truly living in amazing times, my friends." Hercule pressed the clicker again, and the picture changed to an image of a large laboratory. "This is CERN, the foremost particle physics center in the world, where less than one month ago they got their Large Hadron Collider started. The result was far greater than anyone could have predicted and completely disavows the Big Bang theory. They created what is known as *dark matter*. Dark matter was previously thought of as matter that released no radiation and could only be detected by its gravitational pull, but I want you to think of dark matter as the parameters of our universe. Or to simplify things, dark matter is a water balloon, and the universe is the water contained within the balloon.

Dark matter expands to accommodate any form of galactic expansion and creates an environment where particles can create actual matter. Dark Matter is a galactic Petri dish. CERN, with the help of their Large Hadron Collider, has created a new universe."

Hercule stepped back to let the information sink in. "Imagine cell division on methamphetamines. That's what dark matter is capable of. It has endless growth and is a perfect bubble. The universe, in all its diversity of life, is created inside this bubble, and when it needs to get bigger, the dark matter accommodates it and expands to an appropriate size. The universe doesn't expand at any static rate; that's why we had so many problems understanding its expansion. It expands at whatever pace it needs to go."

"What's the point, Lambert?" cried one anxious journalist.

"The point is that inside of that circular container, beneath the contorted amorphous steel and inside this little golden ball, which is a miniature version of CERN's collider, was a globule of dark matter. There is no other place on Earth, except for CERN, that has access to this incredible substance. This, ladies and gentlemen, is a calling card from our intergalactic neighbors!"

One Week Later

Colonel Harp Connors, CERN director Farrokh Dahr, and NASA director Gabe Traffers looked at each other in rapt excitement at the physicist's remarks. The four men walked the gangplank overseeing Ames Research Center's new project, which was headed by Hercule. It was the most ambitious—and thus the most dangerous—project anyone had ever undertaken; but Hercule, with his small stature and squeaky voice, was nothing but confidence.

"Gentlemen ... as you well know, the leading theory of the meteorite that struck earth approximately three weeks ago is that it is a message to us from an alien intelligence." Hercule failed to mention the fact that it was *his* theory. He didn't want his arrogance to get in the way of further grants or the possibility of using Lyndon B. Johnson Space Center to bring his ideas to fruition.

Hercule let his statement hang in the air, letting the information sink in and stew in the three men. He needed to impress them with the progress of his project and with his ability to produce. He especially needed Dhar's approval so he could utilize the Large Hadron Collider and CERN's superior research facilities. Without CERN his project couldn't lift off the ground, but then NASA's support and further grants from the government couldn't hurt either.

"We all know the theory, Lambert. What'd ya bring us here for? The government doesn't have bottomless pockets, you know." Colonel Connors's southern twang tended to make people look past his intelligent eyes. Hercule made a mental note not to disgruntle the man in the future.

"Yes, um, well ... anyway," Hercule stammered and looked to Farrokh who nodded in approval, giving Hercule the steam he needed to continue.

"Well, as you gentlemen know, our planet is unique in our perceivable universe. The chances of life growing on a planet rely on a number of variables, a theorem we call the Goldilocks Principle. The composition of elements, distance from a star, rotation of the planet, lifespan of the star, and plain luck are all components that make up life and must be *just right*," he flexed both index and middle fingers, making air quotes to emphasize his point, "to make life occur. Now, with that being said, do any of you gentlemen have any idea how we could have received a message from a hypothetical life source?"

"No," Colonel Connors said with stony composure, "but you do, so why dontcha stop bein' coy and get to the damn point!" Hercule frowned in disappointment and decided to forego the games.

"Yes. I'm sorry for wasting your time, Colonel. Despite what many people believe, we don't live in a universe, but a multiverse. Imagine a deck of playing cards stacked on one another. Each card is another universe, and each is contained within itself. They never commingle—unless there is an event which makes them." He looked at the men and ignored Connors's consternation. He wanted to make sure they understood, but he was afraid to ask.

"A star collapses on itself, creating such duress that it rips the fabric of space-time connecting the two universes with a portal, otherwise known as a black hole. Think of this phenomena as a needle pushing through two of our playing cards, connecting them."

"Are you saying that this meteorite was not only sent

by an alien intelligence ... but from another universe?" Traffers choked on the thought, and Hercule could tell he was on board. The Americans could now be the first into the next universe. Imagine the funds a president would deliver under such a guarantee.

"Yes," Hercule said, raising his chin a bit. "The exit point of this galactic tunnel would be through what is now called a naked singularity. This is created much the same way as a black hole, except without the gravitational force of the event horizon—just a singularity exposed. Using the card analogy, where the pin pushes through the cards, it creates an indenture, but on the other side, it creates a volcano. The gravity of the black hole forces mass through the indenture and then through the singularity into the other universe. My theory is that in the space between universes you exit your universe through a black hole and enter another through the naked singularity. The key is just finding a way to keep matter protected and in one piece as it passes through."

"You mean like a version of string theory?" Farrokh managed, looking concerned. "This could possibly be the experiment to prove string theory?"

"Yes, we can look at it that way. We have tested the sphere and found that it creates a large magnetic field, forming a gravitational field of such magnitude as to bypass the intense pressure of the singularity. The sphere survives, but the transport doesn't. But what's more important, gentlemen, is that this meteorite came from a naked singularity near the galaxy M51. It came from another universe, traveling through a black hole on their end and exiting the naked singularity in our universe."

The determination in Hercule's face and the weight of his words left even Colonel Connors speechless.

"CERN just created a globule of dark matter, the DNA of the universe, in their Large Hadron Collider. Obviously this alien life is as intelligent as we are, because they were able to build a particle accelerator as well, as evidenced by the dark matter *they* sent *us*.

"My point, gentlemen," he continued "is that they showed us their advancement. Let's show them ours."

"Twenty months ago I had a conversation with three men that forever changed my life and the ideas of physics. I have since become somewhat of a celebrity in the scientific community, as the man who proved string theory. I now stand on the cusp of a much greater journey. The culmination of my forty-four years."

Hercule squinted slightly, trying to cut the glare of the camera lights. It had been five years since his discovery of the meteorite that contained the dark matter. In that span of time, one voyage, Expedition I, had taken place.

Expedition I was a reconnaissance mission to take information from the black hole that Hercule believed to be the entrance to the alternate universe. They took measurements of the gravity pull and size of the black hole and calculated the time it would take to get there.

They also included a globule of dark matter from CERN's laboratories and sent it in a sphere, designed to be similar to CERN's particle accelerator walls. It entered the black hole and was lost on all tracking systems. The voyage was considered a success.

"As some of you may know, just as Expedition I entered the black hole, another meteorite came crashing down toward earth. This again came from the naked singularity by galaxy M51. This *again* was another calling card from our neighbors from the next universe. The sphere was much larger but with cracks interspersed through it. The contained material seems to have been lost to the vastness of space. This, as tragic as it may seem, gives our human race much hope. A civilization as advanced as theirs can still make mistakes."

Camera flashes briefly blinded Hercule, and he raised his hand, blocking the bright lights. He smiled, reveling in satisfaction, before beginning again.

"The sphere held some interesting compounds. The most provocative was carbon, the building block of our existence. Our intergalactic neighbors are trying to speak to us in the inter-universal language of science. Our interpretation of their message is that they, as life-forms, are composed of carbon just as we are. We may be dealing with an alternate universe full of humans. They may actually be having the same press conference as we are. The possibilities are endless. Can you imagine another world filled with human beings on a third planet from some foreign sun, built of carbon, and able to send advanced space expeditions to another universe?" The gentle murmuring in the crowd grew to a cacophony of animated conversation as the people in the audience argued amongst themselves about whether what Hercule had said could possibly be true.

"My mother named me Hercule because of her love for Agatha Christie's famous detective, Hercule Poirot. I'd like to think I have inherited some of his deduction skills and reasoning, and I hope to put all my knowledge forward as I become our first Inter-Universal Ambassador! I will be a primary scientist on Expedition II, which will send a man through an extra-dimensional space to another universe."

When he finished his speech, Hercule took a step back from the podium and then smiled and waved at the cameras and the crowd. His boyish grin and flamboyant wave belied his forty-four years. He walked offstage and was greeted by security guards who ushered him out of the building as various people tried to get his autograph and ask him questions. The paparazzi snapped photos of him as he entered the black limousine. *Finally, the respect I deserve*, he thought as he rode to LBJ Space Center.

"This is Puma Two from Expedition II. All systems go. Ready to pass the point of no return."

Hercule sat strapped in the universal excursion module and thought of the heroic journey he had in front of him.

He could see the black hole swirling in darkness ahead of him, and he felt a twinge of fear. He was sure of his calculations and his ability to solve physics mysteries, but he felt doubt scratching at the back of his mind, like a cat trying to be let in the kitchen door.

"Puma Two this is Capcom. We roger. You are go," Jack Denning answered from Houston. He had never lost a man on a mission, and he didn't want to start now. He stood and looked about the room in appraisal of his hardworking staff, intent on making sure Hercule's trip was a success. His ruminations were interrupted by one of the team's scientists.

"Jack, they found some abnormalities in the most recent sphere!" Paul Stevens, one of the scientists studying the sphere, ran in the room, out of breath and terrified.

"Thank you, Capcom. Main thrusters on," Hercule transmitted.

"What're you doing here, Paul? We're in the middle of a mission!" Jack slid his headphones down to his neck, barely hearing Hercule's transmission. His stomach dropped when he looked into Paul's face.

"It wasn't just carbon in the sphere. It was broken strands of DNA and RNA. Little broken strands of it. At first we were excited. We thought maybe the aliens had sent us forms of their building blocks so we could understand them, but then we started to cross-reference it to figure out what it was and what we could get from it." Paul stared up at the screen at videos of Expedition II speeding up toward the black hole. "It was human DNA."

"So Hercule was right after all. There are humans in an alternate universe trying to contact us." Jack proudly looked back up at the screen and crossed his arms.

"No, sir—" Paul was interrupted by Hercule's transmission.

"I look out into the void of space, and I see a bevy of stars, a universe of possibilities. We stand on the brink of a new life. A life where we are not alone in the cosmos. We can have new neighbors and extend our knowledge of this space we live in. I proudly go where no man has gone before, but with any luck, many will follow. May God be with you all." Hercule finished his aired speech and spoke to Jack one more time. "Jack, I'm opening the sphere now. I'll set the timer to sixty seconds and let you know when I'm entering. Over."

"No! Hercule, wait!" Paul yelled at the screens.

"He can't hear you, Paul. You'd need to be on mic. What is it?" Jack stared at Paul in annoyance. This hardly seemed the time to interrupt, especially since Hercule had passed the point of no return.

"It wasn't just human DNA. When it was put into our formatting computers we found a genetic match for the sample. It was Hercule's DNA." Paul gulped and looked to the screen as the image started to flicker.

"Timer set. Entering sphere."

"I don't understand …" Jack looked in confusion at Paul, who stared at the screen.

"Thirty seconds. Closing sphere capsule door."

"Paul, what does it mean? He's entering a universe of

people who're exactly us?" Jack reached a hand out and touched Paul's shoulder. Paul didn't respond.

"Um ... Capcom, door has a slight malfunction. It's moving slightly slower than it should. Please advise."

Jack looked up to the flickering screen and saw the massiveness of the black hole. He looked to Paul and back at the screen and gently picked up the mic.

"Roger, Puma Two. Try manual override." He dropped his hand and let the mic go.

"Negative ... pcom, sys ... not ... ponding. We ... re at negative ten ... ds. Already in the ... k hole's gravita ... ull. Please advise ... ver." Panic had entered Hercule's voice.

"Oh, my God ..." Paul said softly beside Jack.

"Again, try manual override, Puma Two. Do you copy?" Jack lifted his headphones from his neck and put them back on his ears. He sat down in front of his monitor.

"Nothi ...! ... ressure is ... owering, sphere ... ost close ... ygen leaking!"

"Heart rate speeding up! Temperature cooling!" The biometric monitor yelled across the room.

"System's failing! Oxygen leaking!" cried the systems analyst.

Jack put his hand over his mouth, expecting the worst. The video feed had gone, blinking from a static view of the black hole to nothing. Then Hercule came back on.

"Jack." Paul's voice cracked as he spoke. "It isn't a portal to another universe. It's a time machine!"

Another Ace in the Hole

As Tank walked down the street, ignoring the laughter of the other children and endeavoring to eliminate the hurt of their cruel remarks, he happened upon a card lying in the gutter. It looked old, and its edges were tattered, the face dark from dirt caked into the card's waxy surface. It was an ace of spades, which made Tank feel particularly vindicated and excited. It was the death card, a card that bled power. He ran his hand over the rippled surface and took a deep breath, relishing the thought of warm energy running up his arm from the card.

He was shocked out of his reverie by a rock glancing off the top of his head; laughter reverberated through the air, muffling Tank's cry. They were nothing new to him, these random acts of violence, so he ran forward, ignoring the pain shooting down his back and making an effort to ignore the jeering of the children behind him, all the while wiping tears from his face. Running was never

Tank's forte; however, because of times like these, he did it often. The sight of Tank running was always a surprise because it seemed a boy that big just shouldn't move that fast.

Despite his quickness, Tank was still shocked to escape. In his estimation, children were cruel as a matter of nature, but the only one who resorted to extreme violence like throwing rocks was Ace, the local bully. Tank hated Ace and his cronies; the only thing they seemed capable of creating was misery, and once they started in on you, they usually didn't let you go. But maybe the card was good luck. Usually Ace and his crew meant business if they went as far as to throw rocks.

Tank ran all the way home, clutching the card in his chubby little fingers, praying for deliverance between gasping breaths. Once he was home he didn't stop to pay respects to his mother in the kitchen or plop down in front of the television, as he was prone to do; instead he ran straight for his room, barreling his way up the stairs.

Once in his safe haven he collapsed to the floor, gasping for breath, trying to cover his rosy, wet face. He lay there for an hour, feeling his head for blood and crying to himself about his weight problem. He hated being fat more than he hated the bullies who tortured him. He looked in mirrors and grimaced, knowing the only way to lose weight would be to go on a diet and eat only good foods. He might even have to exercise! The thought made him want to vomit.

After his hour of sulking, he remembered the card,

which he had crushed in his fat little hand. He let out a small squeak, thinking he might have ruined any magic in the card by crushing it, so he bent over it and pressed it on the carpet, hoping and praying the card wasn't ruined, that the crinkles would come out and it would still work.

He was distracted by his mother calling him down to dinner. Any worries about the card or the day's transgressions left him, and he sprinted for the door, whipping it open and shooting down the stairs. Dinnertime was, after all, his favorite time of the day.

Tank's real name was Tanner Miller. The nickname came not just because of the resemblance to his real name, but also because he had a tendency to run over things without noticing them. Tank's mother had taken all fragile knickknacks out of the house because of his clumsiness. *That* was where the nickname had originated, from his penchant for destruction. But it wasn't that Tank was clumsy, though he was; it was that he never quite realized how big he actually was. He would walk by something, thinking he had enough clearance, and run right into it.

Tank was an only child in the Miller household and thus was spoiled all his life, given portions of two instead of one. This could be said to account for his abnormal largeness, but that wouldn't be entirely correct. Tank had a genetics problem; he was born with a damaged thyroid that threw off his metabolism. Somewhere in the back of his mind he knew this and accepted it. It was partly the reason he never fought back against bullies at school—because he knew there was nothing he could do to change it. When his father was still alive, he had told Tank that acceptance of his obesity was the only true way to happiness. Tank fully believed him because his father had been overweight too. Albert Ronald Jackson Miller, or just A.J. for short, had died of a heart attack at the age of thirty-five. Tank's mother had grieved briefly but then turned her attention to Tank to fill the void left by A.J.

Tank's mother was eternally loving and always told Tank he looked great, that he was a "handsome little man." What Tank didn't realize was that Province Miller wasn't saying this out of a mother's love; she just liked larger men—not that she was attracted to her son, she just felt big men were much more attractive.

Province was the one person Tank always felt comfortable around; when he was home she would smother him with care, making him feel truly loved, enabling him to ignore his obesity. She made him feel human, something Tank wasn't used to feeling.

When he went to school he felt like an alien. He knew other people were staring at him. He knew they laughed at him behind his back, sometimes getting bold and yelling out such childish pearls as, "Look out, here comes Fat Ass!" and "Since when did they allow elephants in school?" Tank took much of this in stride and used his imagination to picture their colorful insults. He would imagine he *was* an elephant, walking around in the barren wastelands of the Serengeti, towering above all the small gazelle and prairie dogs, which had his classmates' faces. He dreamed one of them might look up at him and realize they were just two creatures running alone in the desert and ask for his friendship. It never happened. Tank never had any friends, and he always ran home after school.

The next day as Tank was getting ready for school he noticed the card sitting on the floor, a lonely ace sitting on the barren carpet. He reached down and picked it up, rubbing it against his pant leg to straighten it.

He turned and placed it on his dresser as he pulled on his shirt. Once his shirt was on, he put the card in the front pocket, facing in, holding the face of the card to his heart, and then waddled down the staircase for breakfast.

When Tank got to school it was the same routine, kids jeering and yelling obscenities at him. He went from class to class, ignoring his peers and trying to find his happy place, where their tormenting yells could be ignored. His imagination was vast, and it took him to many places; but perhaps his favorite was an amusement park where he could go on all the rides and people would hang out and play with him. Girls batted their eyes at him.

He had been infatuated with amusement parks since he was ten years old. He and his mother had gone for his birthday; his mother had thought it might be good for him to get out and get some fresh air, get on some rides, and forget about his weight problem.

Tank had protested the entire way, so much so that his mother had almost turned the car around to take him home, scolding him for his laziness. She didn't, though, unfortunately for Tank.

When they entered the park, Tank thought it was the greatest place on earth. He loved the loud noises, the conglomeration of people, and the large rides that seemed to fly, but the smells and the food were the best part. He couldn't think of a better way to spend his birthday, and he thanked his mother enthusiastically.

They were at the park for an hour, his mother begging him to go on a ride, when they finally got in line. It all seemed to be in jest, his mother acting like a child, pulling on his sleeve and stamping her feet. Tanner enjoyed the attention, although he did his best to play it off, wanting to give his mother a bear hug to show her his love, unable to express it in words.

The coaster was his mother's choice, a big, twisting thing she was sure he would love. After waiting two hours they got to the front of the line and were getting ready to board. Tanner got in first and crushed himself in the corner of the car, giving his mother room to get in. He wanted her to enjoy herself as he had. He never wanted the smile on her face to wane; conversely he wanted to feel free like a bird with wind whipping around him. His mother got on next to him and gave him a big smile, coercing one out of him as well. It was biggest smile he had ever given; so big it split his lips. Then the attendant came by and tried to close the bar over them—only it wouldn't close. Tanner was just too big.

Province threw a fit, yelling at the attendant; saying he wasn't doing his job and that the manager should come out and they would have words. The attendant apologized, motioning to the safety regulations posted on the wall, and Province grabbed Tank's hand and stormed to the next ride ... with the same result.

With each subsequent rejection Province's face got more and more red, her fists balled so tightly they became white. Tank tried to meekly suggest they should just enjoy the park and forget about the rides, but when she finally started to cry, she turned to him and said, "No one can tell you that you can't do something. They're all being mean. You have to stand up for yourself."

The memory of the smells and campy atmosphere stayed with Tank, not the embarrassment, and he used it as his primary escape. His happy place, somewhere people couldn't hurt him, no matter what they said or did. It was the memory of the place he had been happiest, and it was too strong for others to penetrate.

So when he got to school that day, in his head he went to the park, this time imagining he was on one of the rides, flying through the air with wind blowing through his hair and all his cares far below him on the ground.

But his imagination was so strong he didn't notice Mr. Robertson had been talking to him for a few moments before he recognized Tank wasn't paying attention. Mr.

Robertson got down on one knee in front of him and shook his shoulders, knocking him out of his trance.

"Tanner. Tanner? Are you okay, son?"

"Ye … yes, sir." Tank's hand jumped to his chest pocket to hide the card.

"You were pretty spaced-out there for a minute. I was just giving you kudos for your nameplate."

"Thank you, Mr. Robertson." At first Tank didn't know what he was talking about, but then he remembered the nameplates they had made the week before. Tank had been at the amusement park in his head then as well; he barely remembered making his.

"Don't listen to these kids around here. One day you'll grow up and be their boss." Tank looked into Mr. Robertson's face and gave his best embarrassed/thank-you smile.

It wasn't until after Mr. Robertson walked away that Tank noticed the pocket holding the card was hot. He snapped his hand away as if it were on fire and bent over, letting his shirt fall away from his skin and ignoring the "wide load" jokes coming from behind him.

Tank didn't bother finishing the rest of the day and ran home as fast as his feet would carry him. When he got home he didn't find out if his mother was there. He went straight for the staircase and ran up the stairs to his room, slamming the door behind him and dropping the card to the ground.

In his room he hovered over the card and studied it, trying to find differences between it and normal Bicycle cards. There was nothing out of the ordinary that he could see. His card had the same design as the other cards; it had the same feel and the correct weight. It was just a small playing card that had been lying on the ground.

He got down on all fours and stared at the card. Had it all been in his imagination? Had he needed escape from school so badly that he had made himself think the card had actually heated up?

"Honey? Tanner, baby? Didn't you hear me?"

Tank squealed and turned into his mother's perturbed face, wondering how she had gotten there and why she looked so scared.

"I thought something was wrong! I was about to call the hospital! Are you okay, baby?" The terror faded from her face but was still present, like a ghostly streak left on a pane of glass by a greasy finger.

Tank stared at his mother. *The hospital? Why would she need to call the hospital?* he wondered. He was fine; he had just gotten a scare from the card and was winding down from school. He wondered whether she was angry with him because he had ditched.

"Baby, speak to me. Are you okay?" His mother's voice was frantic and when he looked out the window, he saw why. Had he fallen asleep? How could it be dark outside?

He looked into his mother's eyes and gave her his best smile. He spent long hours in front of his mirror perfecting that look—that "everything is fine" look.

"Sorry, Mom, I didn't mean to scare you. I guess I just

fell asleep. I was really tired, and I found this card outside. I guess I lost track of time." It was the worst excuse he could possibly think up: trite and pathetic, the typical backtracking of a teenager in trouble, but his mother bought it all the same.

"Are you sure you're okay?"

Tank could see relief emerge on his mother's face and hear it in her voice. He had successfully wiped the greasy smear away.

"Yeah, I think I'm just gonna go to sleep. I think that's all I need right now." Tank morphed his expression from a happy, reassuring smile to tired and worn. Once again his mother bought it.

"Okay, baby, but let me know if there's anything I can get you. Just yell down. I'll be listening." She leaned down and kissed his forehead.

"Thanks, Ma," he said, hugging her.

They both got up, and his mother tucked him into bed. He gave her another big smile as she kissed him on the cheek, and he watched as she exited the room. She deliberately left the door slightly cracked before leaving, making sure to give him an "I love you."

Once she was gone Tank sat up in bed and eyed the card on the ground. He gave a little huff of confusion and lay back down, quickly falling asleep.

That was the first dinner he had ever missed.

Tank woke the next morning and left for school after having a hearty breakfast. His mother had woken early, expecting him to make up for lost time, and she had cooked him a feast. He ate ravenously, acting like he hadn't eaten for days, and Province felt relieved as she watched him. How could he remain her sweet little fubsy if he didn't eat?

On his way to school, Tank felt the front pocket of his baggy shirt for the card he had safely tucked there that morning. He wasn't entirely sure why he was bringing it along, especially since it had made him leave school early the day before.

He enjoyed the feeling of the card, though, sitting down low in his pocket. It was like a secret no one else knew about, not even his mother. What kind of powers could the card have? And where had it come from? He thought the power the card surged would only improve his ability to go to his happy place and escape reality, ensuring that he could ignore the real world and all its cruelties. It might even give him the power to make himself skinny and make girls interested in him. Most of all, he thought, it might give him the power to stand up to bullies—to stand up to Ace.

Tank's day at school was moderately long and very boring. When he got to class he immersed himself in work, forgetting he had the card after about twenty minutes of arithmetic. The hours zipped by, but that all changed when school let out for the day.

He left through the gym door on the side of the school, the way he usually did, and made for home; but he only got halfway before the card began to radiate heat again. He was scared at first, remembering how the card had burned his chest the day before, but his curiosity was stronger than his fear.

He reached in his pocket and whipped the card out. He expected to see it glowing a shade of orange, bright with fire, but it just looked like a playing card. Warmth coursed into his fingers, and Tank could only wonder how the card heated up. What kind of magic did it contain? He turned it over, thinking maybe the back held some clue to the mystery.

The back was a dream, white flames leaping, inextricably *there* despite the afternoon glare. He dropped to his knees and slammed the card down on the sidewalk in an effort to put out the flames. He inspected his hands to assess how bad the burn was. Nothing.

He was so taken with the *strangeness* of the situation he barely noticed when a rock skidded off the ground just beyond him. He began to turn to see where it had come from, but before he could, he heard a chorus of taunts: "Look at the fat ass!" and "Don't get too close! He might eat you!"

Tank felt his anger rising, alongside the dread of human interaction he always carried in his heart. Behind him were Carlos Williams, Ben Massey, and Jake "Ace" Wild. Anger fled from Tank the moment he saw them, replaced by intense fear. When these guys decided to bully someone, they didn't quit.

Tank picked up his card, his secret power, and tried to run. But his legs had turned to jelly, and his feet tripped over themselves, flopping him to the ground. He grabbed the card and thrust it into his shirt pocket, trying to ignore the warm waves emanating from it, trying to hide his fear of the three bullies.

"What's that you got there, fat boy?" Carlos squealed, kicking dust and small stones into Tank's face.

Tank immediately pressed his hand to the card to protect it and then promptly scolded himself, recognizing that if they didn't know about the card before, they did now. He pulled his hand back as nonchalantly as he could and put it into the pocket of his slacks.

"Carlos asked you a question, Pillsbury. I expect you to answer," Ace said.

"It … it's nothing," Tank whimpered. He tried to ignore the pain burning into his chest and swore he was going to catch fire. Thoughts of his happy place skittered vaguely around the corners of his mind, but pain focused his mind in reality.

"It's something—otherwise you'd take your hand out of your pocket," Ace said. "I want you to give it before Ben here can count to five, or you're gonna be in a world of pain."

Tank closed his eyes at the onslaught of tears as the gravity of the situation hit him; he had to stop them, or they'd steal his card, steal the source of all that pain and joy. So he opened his eyes and sneered at Ace.

It didn't work.

"Fuck him up."

Ben knocked him down and Carlos kicked him in his ribs, the impact rolling him a few feet away. The boys readied themselves while giving him a chance to stand up and get his bearings. The heat of the burning card spiked in intensity, blazing against his chest, which made him notice something that he never had before.

He was taller than they were.

The three bullies walked toward him, their hands balled in fists, and Tank forgot about the incessant burning. Instead he felt an immense anger well up inside him. He balled his hands into fists mimicking them.

When Ace was in range Tank swung at him with all the strength he had, aiming directly for Ace's stomach, sinking his fist in and doubling him over. But before Tank could manage anything else Ben and Carlos descended, showering his head and shoulders with fists.

When Ace got up, he forgot about the card Tank had been hiding and laid into Tank's ribs with kicks and punches. It surprised Ace that Tank would fight back, and it incensed him more; he wanted to make sure Tank didn't do it again, so he beat him as hard as he could. He beat him until his own hands were bloody; he beat him until Tank went limp. Ace was used to feeling bigger than others; it made him feel like a man.

The last thing that ran through Tank's head was that he had protected *his* ace. He had won.

Tank woke in the hospital, terrified. He was lost, with no idea where he was. The room around him was white and spartan, without any familiar surroundings. He felt for the card, but only found a thin piece of fabric he knew to be a hospital gown. He looked down at his chest, and his head whirled, the room spinning and vomit threatening the back of his throat. He screamed for his mother before he realized what he was doing. Instead of his mother, an unfamiliar nurse arrived.

"What's wrong, honey?" The nurse cooed at him.

"Where am I? What happened?" Countless questions converged in his head, clouding and evaporating his articulation.

"You're in the hospital. You got beat up pretty good; I'm surprised you're awake now. The doctors didn't think you'd be up for hours." The nurse reached out and stroked Tank's hair.

"Huh?" Pain flooded every joint in his body. He felt each individual cut on his face and ribs; every move made each bruise feel like a fist burrowing deep in his muscles.

"You've been unconscious for two days now, honey. It's good to see you awake." She got up and walked over to a table, picking up a small paper cup.

"Two days?" There was no way he could have been out for two days! It had to be a joke; it must've only been a couple of hours. They hadn't beaten him that badly … had they?

"Two days for sure, honey. Your mother has been worried sick. She came in and cried for hours, said she was going to sue the pants off whoever did this to you. Said she wanted to see them in the chair. She went a little crazy."

The nurse put a cup in Tank's hands.

"Why don't you take these now? I'm sure you're in pain. These'll lessen it, make you sleep some." She wiped the hair out of Tanks face and smiled. "Now you get some rest. I'm gonna call your mother, and we'll git her over here as soon as we can." She left the room.

Tank lay there, head spinning, and closed his eyes to try to remember exactly what had happened. But all he could picture was the card. It preoccupied his mind so completely that it was everything outside of the pain. The nurse had said his mother was coming; there was nothing to worry about there. *Where was the card?*

The death card flared in his mind. It was bright white, lending the only light to a backdrop of pure black. Tank felt warm, his gaze transfixed on the card, warmth emanating from it and filling him with pleasure that he had never known, making his loins hum below his large stomach. Tank looked down to see what was happening, why the warmth felt so amazing, but his gut wasn't there anymore. His stomach had shrunk down to a good level, a *respectable* level, and he could see straight down to his toes. But what was even more astonishing and frightening was that, down with all the tingling warmth, his penis stood fully erect.

Tank looked at the card in the inky blackness and saw the glowing shift its focus and shine brightly down upon his groin. The light came off in waves, and as time progressed the waves got brighter and came to him faster. Tank was frightened and tried to turn away, but the sensation the light was bringing was too overpowering. It held him where he lay, making his legs shake and his chest heave.

Tank's back arched, thrusting his groin into the pulsing light. Forgetting his fear, he lost himself in the sensation of the card's light beating down upon him. Pressure was building up inside of him, and he blindly grasped for anything to hold onto while his hips shook. The light pulsated faster and faster, changing color from white to pink to bright red waves.

Tank's strength failed, and he fell back to the bed, spent and sticky, feeling empty and relaxed. Then he started to cry, feeling suddenly guilty—guilty at the act, guilty that it felt good, guilty that he was alone. Something had happened that didn't seem quite right. He felt tears running down his face as he looked back at the card. It was still glowing, but the light switched back to soft phosphorescence as it floated before him. He contemplated the feeling it gave, the feeling of empowerment he had experienced when Ace and the others had attacked him the other day and the sexual comfort it brought him now. He reached for the card and held it against his chest, next to his heart.

The card hummed against his chest, soothing him with its reassuring warmth. He tried to focus on it to relieve the guilt and renew the euphoria, but darkness crept in on him and he slept.

Tank was released the next day. No one spoke of his first wet dream, not to explain what it was nor to berate or console him. To the people in the hospital the wet dream was a normal pubescent function, but to Tank it meant something different altogether. It meant a connection with the card, a link between fantasy and reality. He knew there was something different about that particular, peculiar card. He thought maybe it was made specifically for him, as if it was his own personal savior—something to give him power and make him a man.

When Tank got home, he immediately went to bed, wanting a repeat of the wet dream ... however, none came.

He spent a week at home after he left the hospital, most of it in his room, either sleeping or trying to understand the card. He hardly ate that week, telling his mom his stomach hurt. He would feign vomiting whenever his mother put food in front of him. In truth, he just wasn't hungry. It felt like his stomach had shrunk; he would drink a glass of water and feel full. It was working, too. He had lost twenty pounds since entering the hospital and had never felt better. In fact when he vocalized that he wasn't hungry, he actually *wasn't* hungry. The only time hunger struck him now was when his mother made him eat, restarting his metabolism; and the only reason he complied was that his mother looked haggard. He could tell worry was eating away at her, and he knew the only way to ease her consternation was to eat.

He was complacent in these trivialities; however,

because there was something about the card he had to figure out. The card had levity to it, like a mist that passed through him like an ethereal goddess. Every wave that passed through him felt like ecstasy, more powerful than the caress of a woman's touch. It gave him strength, courage, and discipline. It gave him hope.

The night before he headed back to school Tank had another dream of the card. He had been home for a week and a half, and Province had forgotten all about taking legal action against the people who had attacked Tank. Her fear for his health was just too great.

He had lost thirty pounds and had become merely chubby in his convalescence. Province, eaten up by fear, could only wonder at the cruelties of children. He was once big, so big that people generally didn't bother him, but what would happen when he went to school skinny?

Tank, however, had other, more important things on his mind. In his youth he had yet to find the fairer sex particularly attractive, and the wet dream didn't even really make sense to him. He didn't understand what had happened or what it meant, and it confused him. But when it happened again, he couldn't have been happier ...

Roberta Simmonds. He wasn't sure if that was her name or not; he had never spoken to her, had never even spent more than a couple of moments looking at her, but here she was in all her teenage beauty. He stared at her mosquito-bite breasts and her slightly distended stomach. She stood with a coquettish demeanor, a tinge of smile at the right corner of her mouth, her eyes burning hungrily at his malnourished form, her auburn-blonde hair blowing slightly in a ubiquitous wind. His eyes trailed down her curves until they reached tender, soft peach fuzz, slowly growing thicker the lower he looked. It was uncharted territory; he felt no arousal as he drank her in, just curiosity. That is, of course, until the card came into view.

Roberta's smirk grew larger, and her eyes betrayed her force of desire, a soft white light glowing around her teenage body. Tank felt unsure of himself, unsure of what was expected of him. His stomach dropped, and he felt nauseous, his head swimming.

Her smirk disappeared, replaced by a look of hunger. She no longer looked fourteen; now her body looked older, middle-aged—at least middle-aged to a thirteen-year-old boy. He took a small step back, feeling sweat break out on his forehead along with the emergence of menace into the atmosphere.

It began in his shirt pocket again, intense and localized. Unwittingly his right hand reached up to his pocket and clutched the card. His breath quickened as she approached him. She reached out with her right hand and caressed his ear, while the other hand wrapped around his waist.

He didn't know what to do, what was expected, so he did the only thing that came naturally to him; he took the card out of his pocket, cognizant of his tumescence, and placed it in the center of her chest. Her eyes rolled back, and her mouth formed into an *O*, while he pressed his chest against hers, embracing the heat and channeling his heartbeat to match hers. Tanner felt loss of control in his throat, muttering "ga ... ga ... ga ... ga" in a contiguous rhythm, while pressure built.

He didn't see what happened to her, how she reacted when the cancerous expulsion happened, because he sat bolt upright in bed, holding the card tight in his right hand, encircled around his penis. He felt dampness spread across the blanket and immediately knew it had happened again.

The shame was somewhat lessened this second time, however, as if he had expelled his guilt with the ejaculate. He felt relieved and smiled as he looked around his small bedroom. Today was his first day of school, and he would see Roberta Simmonds, maybe catch a hint of her coy smile. Maybe he would kiss her. Maybe he would ask her to go steady.

Tanner rose from bed and ran across the hallway to the shower, smelling the wonderful fragrance of the full breakfast his mother had prepared. The empowerment he had felt at the end of the dream didn't fade as he washed the semen from his body; it only grew as he donned his previously baggy clothes, which now billowed around him.

He was in such elation that he didn't notice when he slipped the card into the back pocket of his pants. His ace. His wild card.

He went downstairs, smiling more widely than his mother had ever seen. He didn't notice her reaction at the time, mostly because of his levity; but Province seemed to relax when she saw him, and for the first time since his stay at the hospital, she smiled.

Tanner almost finished his breakfast that morning. He honestly tried, but his stomach had shrunk so much, and the breakfast was just too large. He noted his mother's expression, one of fear and tribulation, and smiled meekly as he leaned in to kiss her on the cheek. He wanted to tell her that he loved her and was sorry to cause her any strife, but instead he simply turned and headed for the door.

Outside the air was cold, and he felt goose bumps pop up all over his body. Since he had lost so much weight, his clothes merely caught the wind instead of deterring it, and as a result he shivered his entire way to school. By the time he arrived he felt brittle.

Tanner noted the blank stares of the other students. He knew he looked entirely different, but by most accounts the majority of students hadn't ever seemed to notice him at all, let alone his absence from school.

His will dropped. He had finally begun to think of himself as Tanner, the effulgent Tanner, the one who had lost all the weight; but the apathetic demeanor of his peers destroyed this image, subverting his self-image until he was again Tank the nobody. Tank the fat ass.

He felt joy leak from him, like steam rising from his head, replaced by a much more cold and forlorn feeling.

Did it even matter that he was there? Would he be missed from school? Should he just go?

The front door looked more like the entrance to a prison than a high school; the teachers didn't care, and the students cared even less. No, he'd only be missed if these people needed a punching bag.

He walked over to the curb and sat down, feeling tears well in his eyes. He would suppress it until he knew he was completely alone of course, but the feeling was there nonetheless. When his butt hit the curb he felt a sudden warmth. It surprised him, and he jumped up, swatting at his pants as if he had sat on a fire, but when he stood, the warmth faded. Then he remembered the card.

Elation returned as he shoved his hand into his pocket. His strength returned, and he felt courage pushing out his depression. *Who cares?* he thought. *They don't mean anything to me either.*

He walked through the front doors with gumption and stormed directly to his first class.

That was the first day Tanner felt he learned anything in class. He felt confidence, and it made him see things in a new light. When he looked at the other students, he realized that the looks he had initially taken for disgust were actually obtuseness; they merely didn't recognize him.

Later, when they realized who he was, they congratulated him on his changed appearance. His classmates' compliments amazed Tanner, but what actually got to him was that a select few weren't just being polite—they seemed to really mean it.

He walked with pride in his step, like he was a lord walking among his subjects, and it lasted all day, until it was time to come home. Tanner decided to walk right out the front doors rather than slide out the side door as had been his custom. That was his only mistake.

"Hey, fat fuck, where you goin'?"

Tanner recognized the voice; it was the same voice that played over and over in his mind: Ace. He grabbed the card, squeezing it in his hand and feeling its warmth.

Tanner tensed and stopped walking. He felt pressure build between his shoulder blades, and his stomach clenched; he even curled his toes to give himself extra traction. He had not tested how fast he could run after losing the weight; he fancied himself much faster, but this was not the venue in which he wanted to be tested.

"You gonna talk to me, or are you just gonna stand there, fatty?"

Fire burned in Tanner's palm. He felt it running up his arm and propelling its way down his back, streaming heat through his capillaries. He turned three shades of red, and his face wrinkled, eyes scrunched like a baby throwing a tantrum. He faced Ace.

Ace stood at the top of the steps leading to the building, laughing, his cronies standing on either side of him.

Tanner felt the outline of an *A* burning into his palm, felt it pulsate with power, with heat. Then he saw the loose piece of concrete at the edge of the pathway. It was the size of a large rock and must have weighed at least two or three pounds.

"Oh, look at the baby. I think ... he's ... gonna ... cry!" Ace struggled to finish the sentence, breaking off into such fits of laughter that he leaned over and laid his head on Ben Massey's shoulder.

Everything happened very fast after that. Tank took two running steps toward the bullies, stretching to reach for the concrete, and then taking two more giant, powerful steps. He threw the thing with all his might. He heard his shoulder creak and his muscles rip. He imbued the block with all the heat that had been growing within him, forcing it through his blood into the card and then into the concrete.

Ace lifted his head off Ben's shoulder to taunt Tanner further and, through the worst possible timing, was hit directly above the bridge of his nose.

Ace never felt it crush his skull, but just as quickly as that Tanner ended his reign of terror.

Tanner heard screaming but had no idea what he had done; he only knew that he had fought back. Tanner grabbed his pained shoulder and started to run, wanting to go home, but knowing he couldn't go there. He *knew* Ace was going to get him for this. So he ran to the only place he felt he could be safe, the only place where he could be protected. He ran to the police station.

Tanner was held in protective custody for three days. Province had no idea things had progressed so far for her son, to the point that he would throw stones at other boys. She made a resolution to care for him more, to pay attention to him and nurture his growing needs rather than push her own desires.

Tanner, on the other hand, was worried more about where the card was than about what was going to happen to him. His power, his strength, and his willfulness were directly attributable, at least in his mind, to the card. The attraction to females, the use of his penis for pleasure rather than mere urination, the strength to stand up for himself, and the growth of his self-esteem all now seemed to be void in its absence. Guilt filled that void—more even than the guilt of his first wet dream—because he had ended someone's life. As much as he felt he had done a service to mankind with the dispatching of Ace, he felt *cold*.

On the fourth day Tanner's mother took him to school. He sat in the car with his head lowered, depressed and terrified of what his classmates would do to him.

The school rose in the window, and a vision of what this place had meant to him before came back to him; it looked like a prison. He'd be stuck here all day without the protection offered by the police or the comfort of his mother. He'd be alone.

They pulled up front, and Tanner grabbed for his backpack in the backseat, sighing as he did so. Province grabbed his arm and forced him to look at her.

"Tanner, you're a man now. Be good." She nodded as if to give meaning and purpose.

Province meant that, after what he'd been through, other children at school would either be scared of him or would look up to him. He was a role model now whether he liked it or not; he had to be careful to show his contrition.

Tanner took his mother to mean that now that he had killed he was a man, and that gave him the power of fear, which Tanner took as a burden. He sat with the backpack now pulled into his lap and thought about it. He had once been terrified of those kids, what they would do, what they would say, and rather than push through it, he had become shy. Now it was his peers who would feel the fear. He had to be careful because now *he was Ace*.

Ben Massey and Carlos Williams were standing in front of the school, waiting for him. When Tanner saw them he paused and said a prayer as they walked over.

"Hey, Tanner! Um … hey!" It was Carlos.

Tanner stopped and stared as the two bullies closed the distance. His eyes scanned the few students milling around before the bell rang, in hopes of finding someone to interject, at least long enough for the bell to ring. But no one was looking—except for Roberta Simmonds. She had a disgusted look on her face and spit in his direction before whipping around and storming off. One thing repeated in his mind: he was Ace now.

"Tan the man." Ben laughed. "I was wonderin' …" he began as he closed the gap. Tanner could only imagine what these two were up to—the two who had beaten him to the point of unconsciousness. They seemed amiable now, as if they were scared of him, but he couldn't be sure.

"What's up?"

"Hey, dude ... you should, you know ... like, let us, kinda, follow you?" It shouldn't have been a question, but there was undoubtedly a raise at the end of his sentence. Tanner thought back to what his mother had said in the car. He *was* taller than they were.

"Anytime."

Tanner looked past their relieved faces, searching for Roberta, but she had gone. Instead his eyes caught Darla Wallace. Darla? She *was* prettier than Roberta. His now only *slightly* chubby cheeks rose into a smile, and he ascended the small staircase that led to the school. He glanced down at the spot where Ace had been standing when he was hit. Down at the side of the staircase was a playing card. Its face was down, so he couldn't tell what it was, but it looked old and well loved. It looked like his ace. Tanner glanced at Carlos, who was looking at him reverentially.

"Leave it. You don't need it," Tanner said out loud, thinking of his mother's words and then of Ace's malicious sneer. *I'm a man now.*

The Barn Burner

I watch her drive away. The anger sifts off my head, rising like steam. The room is frigid, and the tension is palpable. I walk back to the bar and take a plastic bottle of bad whiskey. I have a barn burner planned. The twelve-pack of Budweiser in the fridge is calling to me.

I whip open the freezer and pull out ice cubes, relishing the ample cold pouring from inside. I drop the ice cubes in a glass, splash in the whiskey, and down it, barely a sheen on the cubes before the alcohol is gone.

"That bitch." Not properly directed anger, it could have been toward the woman who cut me off in traffic earlier; but no, I am talking of her. My angel. My love. That bitch.

I know my brain when in a state of anger. Moral consciousness is absent, leaving only pure rage. The fire that burns in my head is outstripped only by the passion that fills my heart. I have plenty of both. I sometimes believe these are the only attributes I have, fire and passion, and I ponder the social aspects of such drive. I wonder why girls keep coming to me.

I don't see beauty in the mirror. I see a scorched constitution. I see a boy who is so unsure of himself that when girls approach, it's an all-or-nothing deal, a forged contract. Alcohol disarming their tractor beams, leading them astray ... into my arms. This humble self-discord leaves naught for the imagination. If girls make the first move, I must accept; it may be my last opportunity to find real love. But that's not the real reason, is it? I desire to be desired. A kiss is the fire that drives my passion.

Discord permeates my skull. I know what I am doing, and at the same time I don't. I relish the anger and frustration; it gives me solace, yet I feel that discordant beat in my heart that tells me I loved her. She came to me. She loved me. That has to mean something.

It meant cold exhaust wafting into my lungs, while I watched her drive away. A lump in my throat.

"What the fuck!" Anger distills my emotion to monosyllabic words, only adding second syllables for emphasis. "Fucking bitch!"

I start to pace, aimlessly, my purpose only to walk, to blow off steam. The anger has risen so high that I can't even think.

What was she thinking? How could she drive away so calmly and serenely? I'd like to think of her sitting there with her bug-eyed glasses blocking the tears billowing at the edges of her lids, but I know she feels no despair. That would only be too great; it's too marvelous a thought. No, she's zoned out, looking at the road but not seeing it, planning her next PETA meeting. Sure, she can be ethical toward animals, but when it comes to a man she says she loves, she'll fuck the nearest living thing.

Carbon life, trite but true. Think about the person in front of you one day. Think about being inside of her, being behind her eyes, feeling the frailty and deficient form that constitute the human body, and knowing in actuality that there is nothing better about her, that she's made of the same material. She's as easily hurt as you. Flesh is flesh.

Or better yet, think of her as a baby. A small child suckling at her mother's teat, totally innocent, devoid of any malignant imposition that would enable the brain to formulate evil and replicate it. This child is what she was—what she still *is*. Flesh is flesh after all.

That line of thinking should have been enough to get me out of my slump, to forget; but by the time it formulated I had already had three swigs of whiskey. Bad timing, I guess.

"Fucking *bitch*!" I'm still stretching for emphasis.

I'm lucky because I haven't broken anything yet. That tends to be a predisposition of mine. Either that or punching walls, but I prefer to retain the use of my hands.

I accept the fact that I have character defects; I just don't think that other people should. Throwing things seems like a perfectly succinct way for a cuckold to express that, doesn't it?

"Fucking drove away!" I can still taste the exhaust. Bland and burning. It tastes like rejection.

I throw back my head and pour the remaining beer down my throat, crushing the can in the process. I stumble back a step and throw it at the wall, creating a of clatter about as abrasive as a couple of dice rolling across a table. Great fucking effect.

I stop myself, my anger abating, when I realize just how ridiculous I look—like a horrible B actor trying his best for an Oscar. I hope to God no one is looking in the windows.

"Fucking bitch."

Heavily scented air filled the bar. I saw her enter, wearing a thigh-high dress with jeans on underneath. Why the hell do I find that sexy? There was a cool breeze blowing behind her, gently tossing her hair about her head. She was wearing an unbuttoned blue peacoat, and a streetlight shined behind her, casting a halo about her head in soft, warm light.

"Goddamn." The guy next to me whipped his head around, drunken eyes wavering in their sockets. I wasn't sure if he was looking at me or the bartender.

"Thas right. Goddamn it!" He spit as much as he slurred. "Whas it *take* to fucking drink 'round here?"

He put his hand on my shoulder, a gesture of friendship, of companionable fortitude in the face of a packed bar. I smiled gently and pushed it off, nodding and looking back for the bartender intently. She had sidled up beside me at the bar, and I hadn't even noticed.

Looking back, I realize there was only one possible entrance for her. The bar was busy, and the person who had been sitting on the stool next to me had gotten up to take a leak. When she sat down I could *feel* her there, as if she was giving off radiation.

My mouth was suddenly dry. Her auburn hair was ruffled from the wind, and her cheeks were rosy, not from makeup, but from the cold night air. Her lips were full and red, not overtly, but with a slight sheen that reflected the light and showed their fullness.

I took a long drink of whatever I was drinking, hoping the quaff would alleviate my inhibitions. Liquid courage. I tried to lean my body ever so slightly so as to turn more toward her, get her attention. But I made a slight miscalculation. The stool I was on was precariously balancing on the edge of a step, and by moving so briskly, I managed to plunge the stool off the edge, plummeting myself off the stool and onto the hardwood floor of the bar. Excellent first move.

"Shit!" The parameters of intelligence only encompass times of mental inaction. It's very hard to say anything intelligent when you're drunk and falling off a stool in front of someone who takes your breath away.

She was on me before I knew I hit the ground. I felt her soft hand press against my cheek, a gesture of concern. I opened my eyes, gazing into clear, deep pools—hazel with a tint of the sky swirled in. Kind eyes, with only a hint of smile around the edges. She knew I was embarrassed, but she didn't take advantage.

"Are you okay?" Breathy diction with smooth intonation. Sexy.

"Umm …" Fear and anger work the same way. In the throes of either, only one syllable emerges.

"Is that a yes?" Her smile revealed itself, and her hand moved from my cheek around to the back of my head. I felt her fingernails sweetly scratch through my hair. It took all my nerve not to reach up and hold her against me, to feel her heart beating close to mine, to smell her lavender-scented hair and strawberry breath, to keep that comfort completely encompassed in that embrace, that memory. Instead I slowly stood up.

"Wow, that wasn't embarrassing or anything." I could feel my ears burning. I envisioned my cheeks turning scarlet, especially where the memory of her hand still lingered.

The whiskey is half gone, and there are four empty beer cans lying in front of me. I didn't spend the time to right them when they fell over. They *all* seemed to fall over. It didn't matter which way I put them on the table. Defective, all of them. Why the fuck can't I get anything to stay upright? Do I have to slam a fucking pole through them and pound it into the table? And, yes, by the way, I realize how ridiculous this sounds, being angry at the fucking beer cans, but where else should my anger lead me? I don't want to think about her. I don't want to think about her betrayal.

I long for solace, so I look to a giant painting of an old ship I have on the wall. It is something my grandmother gave me, and with it came an insatiable wanderlust. I remember a deep longing to be on that ship as a child, to ride along with the sailors and pirates, never to be held down in one place, never having to worry about paying bills. Just me, a couple of other seaworthy men, and the open sea. Nothing to fear but death. I feel peace when I look at this painting; there are worlds outside of my own, outside of this beautiful but torturous relationship, places where I can be at peace.

I'm pulled back from my wonderment by the sound of a can falling over.

"Fucking bitch!" I'm not sure if I'm talking about her or the can. Hell, at this point I don't think it matters. She's ruined my life, and I'm in hell. Not only did she cuckold me, but *she* left *me*! I didn't even boot her out the door!

I reach into the cabinet and grab the shotgun. I lay it against the couch and head back to the fridge for another beer. Funny, they call it a barn burner. I would like that, yes. Burn down that fucking barn.

She held my hand the entire night, the warm compress of her palm against mine, with only the slight dampness of impending sweat. I felt comfortable, conjoined, as if I was stronger with her attached to me, even if we were only connected through our hands.

I saw her nervousness in her feet first. On the drive back to her house I could see them jittering, as if moving to a silent beat. The talk was light and pointless, about the movie we had just seen, *The NeverEnding Story*. We were both ignoring the fact that she had balled her eyes out when the horse was dragged into the swamp. I could see the embarrassment in her eyes, deep and ingrained.

She had a purple coat on that night, matching the sunset. I looked at her image, framed by the orange-purple light, and she was perfect. Her cheeks were slightly rosy, reminiscent of the first time we met, and her eyes were soft from the tears that had watered them earlier. During the movie, she had wiped away her makeup with my handkerchief, and it gave her an ethereal glow, her natural, soft face against the dramatic backdrop of all the colors of the sunset. She smiled when I looked at her, coy and shy all at the same time. I'm intimating that it was because she thought I was attempting to ascertain the reason behind her forlorn demeanor. In actuality, it was because in that exact moment, with the dying sun lighting her up, putting fire in her hair, emphasizing the tenderness in her gaze, with her purple jacket framing her petite body against the fading of the light, she looked like an angel. Her hand, that warm, damp compress, was the only thing to give me the illusion of reality. And the more intently I stared at her, the tighter the grip became.

I felt a surge of energy float up from my hand, through

my arm, and into my heart, flowing into my blood stream, flowing through my blood vessels. It was as if she were giving me an infectious disease. I could feel the energy coursing through my body, a levity, a lightheadedness, a rush of joy. My heart entered my throat, causing my tongue to stick in place. The only words I could manage to convey my feelings came when I dropped her off at her doorstep.

I looked at the barn behind her house. I smiled at her. "Thank you."

My mouth hung open for a moment after I spoke the words, as if I was going to say more, but when nothing came I smiled again.

She, however, didn't answer. She just jumped at me and hugged me with fierceness, like she was trying to squeeze me in half, destroy my body, and hold onto my soul. My heart leaped again and she felt it, the loud thump against her breast caused an echoing rhythm in her. And she hugged *tighter*.

She moved her head from my neck; I could hear and feel her intake of breath. I looked into her eyes and watched as she bit her lower lip, eager, her eyes provoking.

I lost reason. I lost lucidity. I lost hope. Her lips touched mine, and I forgot how to live my life alone.

I gaze down into the barrel of the shotgun. She has a cute little name for him. A pet name. She calls him the Italian Stallion. Too fucking cute for words. He isn't even Italian.

Two thirds of the bottle are gone, along with two more beers. I have a vague recollection of what the problem is, but at this point I pretty much only feel anger.

"Sherb fook, haarry prick."

Flailing blindly around the room, the only thing keeping me alive is the fact that I didn't load the shotgun. I'm not entirely sure if I could load it at this level of drunkenness.

I know at some point I tried to fire it. I think I blacked out. I think I'm pissed. I think I need to burn her barn. That beloved fucking barn where all her indiscretions took place. That fucking barn where she made a cuckold of me. That fucking barn was where all the damage came from. Fuck the barn.

I had planned a barn burner tonight, but now that phrase has taken on a whole new meaning for me. Fuck her, and fuck that barn.

The shotgun drops from my hand with a perfunctory thud. I make my way to my garage and grab my spare tank of gas, which just so happens to be resting snugly against the back hatch of my Jeep. Fucking divine providence.

I was watching football when it happened—ignorant to the indiscretion, the blind *cheating* that was about to be unloaded on me.

"Baby, I need to talk to you."

I felt a hand on my shoulder, warm and soothing. A

surge of warmth flew through me, straight to my heart, brightening my disposition. I turned and looked into her azure-hazel eyes, with tendrils of color weaving into one another, creating a slight marble effect. There was consternation in her expression; she pursed her lips. My thoughts turned black with that quintessential expression: "Uh-oh!"

"What's wrong, baby?" I reached behind me with my right arm and caressed her forearm, hoping to coax fortuitousness. "Come over and sit down."

"No, I'd rather stand." It was a quick answer. I knew I was in trouble.

"Disclose."

She didn't answer at first; she just sighed and walked around in front of me, in front of the TV. She was indicating I was to give her my full attention.

"I don't know …"

I grew impatient with her game. "Babe, I know you like to be coy, but just say what's on your mind. We'll get through whatever."

"No, I don't think so."

My heart dropped and skipped a beat. Not this talk, not with her. Please, God … not with her.

"What …?"

"I'm leaving." She stopped as if I would say something in response, as if I could respond. "I've … found something. Someone." She was quick to correct herself.

I think I tried to speak. I tried to come up with something intelligent to say. I wanted to be Humphrey Bogart.

Instead I said, "Where?"

"It's been in the barn, only a few times, but I can't go ba—I mean it's unlike anything ..."

I stayed silent a second time. Then the nausea hit, and I ran for the toilet. I retched three times. It was a horrible feeling. There was nothing in my stomach, but it was clenching like vise grip. I heard her in the hall behind me.

"I know it's coming as a surprise. It was for me, too, but it's just so damn *good*."

I retched harder. I could feel my intestines moving upward.

"What's his name?" I managed between retches. I reached up to the toilet tank cover trying to raise myself, the horrible clenching of my stomach slowly subsiding.

"Paulo. He's beautiful and exotic. He's from Andalusia. He's just so ... I mean we have this connectedness ... I just can't go back. He's just such a beautiful man."

My stomach wrenched again, but I didn't throw up. I shit myself. And I screamed more than I thought possible. She left in a hurry. I thought of the drink in the kitchen. I had to plan a barn burner, as much as I could drink. I would *have* to stay up all night. I had a barn to burn, and with any luck it would be occupied.

The Sniper

Roger Tambour climbed the hill like a lynx hunting its prey, sweating from the weight of his pack and the heat of the desert sun. The intelligence he had gotten from his informant told him his mark would be bartering a deal in twenty minutes two hundred yards south of the hill he was climbing. He had just enough time to crest the hill, settle, and then facilitate the kill—such effort for that single beautiful moment when his rifle, the impeccable extension of his arm, bucked against his shoulder and the mark would be felled. There was no *semper fi* in this business, no glory, no gung ho motherfuckers. Just Roger and the pop of his rifle echoing, indicating the hollow void it brought.

"Boy, you shut that goddamn animal up, or you gonna make me do something about it!" Pete Tambour leaned out of his La-Z-Boy and craned his neck into the living room where Roger was playing. "I'm serious now. I've *eaten* mangier in Vietnam!"

Pete was an absentee father. He was only around for about a week a month. Roger's mother, Patricia, told him his father traveled for work, but he always came home stinking of booze and cheap perfume.

Roger slowly got to his feet, putting his arms out for balance. He had just turned four and was still a little wobbly on his feet.

"Shit, boy, you need to learn your balance." Pete turned back to the television and carefully lifted a Bud to his lips.

Roger waddled over to the small collie puppy rolling on its back next to his father's chair. His mother had named the dog Spunky.

"You stupid, lazy, fat piece of shit!" Patricia stormed into the room, waving a letter in her hand. Roger stood on his little fat legs with a look of surprise at his mother's sudden entrance. The dog barked in response to Patricia's tone.

"You talking to me, baby?" Pete said, not taking his eyes from the television.

"What the fuck is this?" She stood in front of him, waving the letter with a hand on her hip.

"Jesus, woman, you're worse than the dog," Pete said taking another swig of beer. He didn't move but slightly raised his eyes to meet hers.

Spunky stopped rolling around and turned to face the drama, giving a sharp, high-pitched bark.

"Get that fucking mutt out of here, Roger." Patricia

turned to her son with her eyes burning and then turned back to Pete. "Is this a fucking pink slip?" she asked, rustling it in his face again.

Roger looked down at the dog and then back up at his mother. They'd freed him from the pound a month earlier, and Patricia had said it was the most beautiful creature she had ever seen. It was one of the best days Roger had ever had.

"What the fuck you think it is? It's pink, ain't it?" Pete gave a wry smile and stared deep in her eyes.

"So, let me get this straight … you don't clean, you don't take care of the children, you can't get it up, and now you aren't even working?" Now both fists were pressed to her hips, and the letter was crumpled in her hand.

"Huhm," Pete said, raising his eyes thoughtfully and rubbing his chin. "Looks about that way, doesn't it? Well, except for the getting it up. It's hard to fuck a bitch while she's complaining the entire time."

"Fuck you! I'm done, you piece of shit!" She threw the letter at Pete, turned, and walked out the door. It was the last time little Roger saw his mother.

"What got up her ass, huh?" Pete said, turning to face Roger. "You gonna get that thing out the room or not, boy? *Jeopardy*'s on."

Lookout duty. It was the slowest task in the barracks, and Roger resented Sven for making them pull it. Their job was to watch the access road that led to the barracks and shoo away any visitors. Out of ten shifts Roger had only seen one civilian approach the gate, and when he realized where he was, the man had quickly turned and walked away.

It was a slow time, when you got to know the guy you were with because there wasn't anything to do other than talk. So there they stood, rifles at their sides and faces showing the torture of boredom.

"Fucking dog," Sven spat out. Roger didn't respond but turned to look at his comrade.

"Don't look at me like that, man! Fucking thing had it coming, and you know it! Fucker bites!" Roger didn't know the whole story and wasn't sure if he wanted to. All Roger knew was that they were pulling head duty together when Sven had wandered off. Then the sergeant's dog was found dead under the steps of C Company's barracks.

"Fuck, it's like he could smell it on me, man." Sven started to violently scratch his head. It was the part of the army that always pleased Roger. He didn't know about Sven's past, and he wasn't particularly interested; but he knew it was checkered. "Like he could smell the fucking thing's saliva. I swear, man, that his nostrils actually *flared* as he was looking me over. Thought he was gonna cry."

Roger was glad to have Sven next to him, glad that Sven was in the same company because it lessened the chance that he would ever have to stare down a rifle at him. Lessened.

"You got any grass, man? I need to relax." Sven

fidgeted and swung his rifle over his shoulder, bending to tie his shoe. "Tell you what, man. I'm gonna go over there by the fence and jack one. You stick here and keep your queer-boy eyes to yourself, got it?"

When dealing with Sven, Roger realized the best recourse was to say nothing and let Sven assume your answer. He took silence for acceptance.

While Sven was doing his business, Roger leaned back and drank in the clear blue skies. It was a beautiful day, and it reminded him of his first day in the army, when he knew for sure that he had escaped from his family—from his drunkard father, from his sister who worked herself into the ground to pay for everything for their family, and from his younger brother, who had discovered meth and began to steal from his sister's purse.

He walked out into the cool air and felt his first breath of freedom. He vowed he would spend his whole new life trying to forget his old one.

"Shoulda fucked the dog first before I killed it," Sven said, walking back over, buttoning up his trousers as he did so. "Coulda released some of the tension in my shoulders."

Sven smiled a crooked, snaggletoothed grin and patted Roger on the shoulder. "Bet you think killing a dog is a rush. Just wait till we get over to Iraq. There's gonna be a storm in the desert for sure, and that fucking storm is of Norwegian descent."

Despite his vulgar behavior and his bravado, Roger saw intelligence behind Sven's eyes. Brutal and honest.

He knew in that moment that he could never cross Sven, because Sven would never give him a second chance.

Roger gently cocked his head to the side to look through the scope. The pudgy white man was centered in the crosshairs as he brokered whatever transaction he had set up.

Roger took out his DEA-issued pen and wrote down a short description of the contact: "Tall, skinny, white woman. Thirty-five. Brown hair. Strong handshake, confident body language."

Roger took a deep breath and gently placed his finger over the trigger. He began to say the prayer he had learned from the Norwegian sniper who had died in his arms. He began a countdown in his head, all the while keeping the short, pudgy man in his kill zone.

"Boy! Another F! I ain't raising no dumbasses! What's this all about?" Pete stumbled out of the kitchen, waving around Carl's report card.

They had lived in a sty ever since Patricia had walked out on them. They never received a note from her; she never called to ask how they were doing. It was just Katie, Roger, Carl, and their drunken father.

"You hear me, boy?" Pete drooled as he spoke. It had

been three years since Pete had held a job, and he'd had a beer in his hand nearly the entire time.

Carl never heard his father stumbling around the house because he was holed up in his room listening to Pink Floyd, high as a kite and trying to forget his life. He had taken "Comfortably Numb" as his anthem the year before. He had shrunken in on himself and refused to speak about anything but superficialities to everyone except Roger.

When Pete burst into the room, Carl didn't have time to hide the marijuana in the baggie on his bed, but luckily, in his drunken stupor, Pete sat on it without noticing.

"What's up, Pete?" Carl had just turned thirteen and had long since lost any respect for his father.

"You shouldn't call me that," Pete said, losing his steam and forgetting why he had come into the room.

"It's your name, isn't it?" Carl's rejoinder was icy.

"Why don't you call me Dad?" Pete said, raising his arm to ruffle Carl's hair. Carl moved out of the way.

"I'll try to do that." Carl's gray eyes stared back into his father's dull blue ones. "I'm gonna take a nap now, 'kay?" Carl said without even faking a yawn.

"Naw, why don't you come out and watch TV with your pops?" Pete reached out again, and again Carl deftly moved out of the way.

"No. I think you need to talk to Roger. He said he was going into the army," Carl said in a monotone. He didn't think it would get his brother into trouble, and he wanted to be rid of Pete.

"What?" Pete said swaying on the bed.

"Yep, spoke to a recruiter. They said in two years, when he turns eighteen he'll be a shoo-in." Carl got up as he spoke and walked to the head of the bed, pulling the sheets aside.

"Fuck, you say!" Pete got up, knocked the weed to the ground, and stormed out of the room. "Rog!" he yelled out into the house.

"Pete, will you knock it off?" Katie yelled back at him from the kitchen. She was going over rental units because she couldn't pay the mortgage to the house and the collectors had started calling.

"Don't you call me Pete! You call me Father!" Pete yelled as he stumbled back down the hall. In the past three years he had put multiple dents in the weak walls during his drunken meanderings.

"Why don't you act like a fucking father, you asshole?" Katie said under her breath. "And by the way, Roger isn't home. He's off playing in the park."

Pete made it into the room and threw down Carl's report card, stomping on it in the process.

"Playing in the fucking park? He's sixteen goddamn years old. He's too old to be playing in the park!" Pete said, making his way toward the refrigerator. "You fucking kids drive me to drink!"

"That's why you do it? I didn't know." Katie didn't mask her condescension.

"Goddamn right." Pete took two beers from the fridge and took them to the living room to his favorite seat in front of the TV, the argument forgotten.

Katie wrote a quick note to Roger, posted it on the refrigerator, and then went into Carl's room.

"I'm going to find a way out of here, Carl," she said from the doorway.

Carl was sitting at the window, looking out into the midafternoon gloom. "Whatever." He didn't turn around.

"These Iraqi motherfuckers aren't gonna know what hit 'em." Sven chuckled as he cleaned his rifle. The two of them had gone into sharpshooter school together and had done fairly well. Sven was a natural. He didn't seem to ever miss, right from the beginning of the training. The mark could be running; they could be hiding—Sven never missed. He was a killing machine, and he was never happier than when he hit his target.

Roger, on the other hand, struggled. His hands were a shaky bundle of nerves, and he had trouble understanding how to lead the mark. As Sven continued to excel, Roger became increasingly determined. As time in camp grew longer, so did the war. He knew it was only a matter of time before his squad was called into battle, and he knew he needed to pass his sniper exam. There was no way he was going to war without Sven the killing machine at his side. Despite knowing, clearly, that Sven was a sociopath, Roger never felt more comfortable than when he was in his presence. He knew Sven thought of Roger as a friend, because Roger had accepted him for who he was, even with knowing about Sven's homicidal tendencies.

In the real world their friendship would have never blossomed, and Roger knew it. He would never tell Sven that, though, because he didn't know if Sven realized that the only reason Roger felt comfortable with him was because they had a common enemy. There was direction for Sven's psychosis; without direction, Roger didn't know what Sven would do.

"You're telling me. They walk by a building with Sven the killing machine in it? They're gonna be red paste on the sidewalk!" They would banter for hours, each trying to top the other's crudeness, both ignoring the fact that the next morning they were going into a city where the enemy outnumbered them three to one.

Roger flattened himself on the ground, zeroing in on the mark. He thought back to his training. He thought about Carl playing shooting games with him in the arcade when they were kids. He thought of Sven and how similar their families' actions were. He thought about Katie and how she was working with a lawyer in New York now. He thought about Carl in jail. He thought about the abuse of his mother and father. He thought about the connection he had with Carl and Katie, and he felt a tear roll down his cheek.

He looked down at the chubby man through the scope

and realized the man was looking at him—had in fact winked at him—and Roger's tears poured. He paused, his finger waiting for the tears to clear and his vision to return so he could gaze back into Carl's gray pleading eyes.

Roger turned back to Sven as soon as he saw the Iraqi soldiers retreating.

The bullet had taken Sven by surprise just a moment before, piercing his jugular and knocking him back on his ass.

"Ohfuckohfuckohfuckohfuckohfuck." Sven kept repeating the words, his hand clamped on his neck.

"Medic!" Roger yelled and ran to his fallen friend.

"Shit, man! Fucker got me!" Sven's skin had already paled.

"You'll be all right. Fucker just got lucky, man," Roger said, putting his hand over Sven's, increasing the pressure on Sven's neck.

"Bitch hurts, man. Can't believe how lucky that guy got!" It was always luck when an Iraqi shot an American, but skill when an American shot an Iraqi.

"Yeah, fucking Sunday fighters don't have a chance. Don't know why they're even trying." Roger could feel the pulse of Sven's blood against his hand. He could also feel Sven's hand weakening.

"Man, it's fucking cold in here. You got any water?" Sven's eyes became glossy.

"Fuck! *Medic!*" Roger couldn't hide his impatience as he felt the blood rushing between Sven's fingers.

"Cool it, man. Cool it. It's too late."

Roger looked back down at his comrade and felt panicked. "Don't you give up! I need your crazy ass to keep me alive."

"You'll be all right. Remember the prayer. It'll calm you," Sven said. His hand released its grip and only stayed in place because Roger was holding it there. "Remember our families brought us here. We can party in hell when you die."

"Quitter! Fuck you! I ain't goin' to hell!" Roger screamed in his dead friend's face.

"I'm taking him out of here, Rog. I'm sorry, but he needs freedom from this place." Katie sat on the bed, stroking Carl's hair, while Roger stood in the doorway.

He had known this was coming, but he couldn't bring himself to give Katie his prepared speech. He wanted to tell her they needed to stay together. He wanted to say they needed each other's support. Instead he just stood there, nodding at her.

"When I heard him come home, I got out of bed and went up to check on him. By the time I got there, he'd thrown up on his bed and was lying in his own filth." Roger looked down to his snoring brother and then back at his big sister. "He had two thousand dollars in his pocket, Rog. He's selling this shit now."

Roger looked one more time at Carl. He took note of Carl's emaciated form, the blood stains on his upper lip from his bloody nose, the sweaty, tousled hair, and Roger came to his own conclusion.

"We have to get out of here. Carl can't stay here any longer. He needs to get away from that asshole." She nodded her head toward the living room to indicate Pete. "He needs to get clean, and he needs to stop getting abused. Were going to New York. It's far enough away from here that I don't think he can find us. Let the bastard rot."

Roger turned and looked at the door leading to the living room. Then he looked back at his sister, and the realization of Katie's words struck him all at once. They all needed emancipation.

"I can't go with you." His words were soft and quiet. He dropped his eyes as he said it, feeling shame blush his cheeks.

"You have to go with us. I need help with Carl. It isn't going to be easy getting him off this shit." He could see anger creating creases at the corners of her mouth, and his shame blossomed enough to change his complexion.

"I can't do it. I'm not going with you." Roger slowly raised his eyes to meet Katie's. He could see the hurt in her eyes.

"Fine. We don't need you. We lived for years with that pig"—she motioned with her head toward the living room again—"without your help, so we don't need it now."

He didn't respond, just looked at her. He felt the

shame, but he didn't feel remorse. He knew he had to get away from them. Things would never change if he stayed near them. They would always control his emotions; they would always control his actions.

"Well, no reason to wait. Why don't you get out of here so I can get us packed, huh?" She didn't meet his eyes, but she nodded at the door again.

Roger acquiesced and joined his father in the living room, pulling a brochure out of his back pocket in the process.

In big block letters at the top it said: An Army of One.

Roger could see Sven on the other hill three hundred yards away. He knew Sven never hesitated, even in such blaring heat with sweat pouring in his eyes.

The rifle rested on its stand, and he relaxed his shoulders. He wished the prayer that Sven said before every kill worked for him like it did with Sven. It seemed simple, but it also seemed to relax him. Sven had ten confirmed kills. Roger had none. But down there in the valley was an Iraqi guard whom they were sent to kill, and Sven refused to do it this time.

"You're making me the default," Sven had said. "You need to do this one. You with me?"

It wasn't that Roger didn't want to do it—he was aching to. He needed a release for all the pent-up anger he had brewing inside him, but every time he went to pull the trigger, he jumped and missed wide, leaving Sven to make the shot and finish the job.

"Say the prayer, man. I know you ain't religious, but that shit works. My anticipation goes away, and I can take a deep breath and finally just get to it."

Despite what Sven said, the prayer only took his mind off the guard for a moment. The anticipation was still there, and the excitement would lead his fingers.

He focused through the scope and centered the guard's head in the crosshairs. He could see the man's brown eyes and the wrinkles in his face. He had to be in his fifties. Anger suddenly surged through Roger, and he pulled his finger off the trigger before he fired astray.

"Who the fuck are you?" he muttered under his breath at the guard. Images of beating the guard ran through his head. Breaking the man's nose. Cracking ribs. Stomping his fallen form.

Then suddenly the man became Pete, and Roger nearly jumped up and charged. He ripped his face away from the scope and took a few deep breaths.

"Just calm down. Just do it," he whispered to himself.

He focused on the guard one more time, took another breath, and pulled the trigger. The bullet was true, and the man fell immediately; but Roger felt emptiness creep into him. His first confirmed kill, but there was nothing to it, nothing personal. The man was just a notch on the side of a rifle. Roger's anger grew.

Carl said goodnight over the phone to Katie. He told her he was in his room in the recovery clinic, but in actuality, he had left two days before and had been traveling nonstop since. He hitched rides and rode buses where he could, and where none were possible, he walked.

His doctor in the clinic told him his drug habit had arisen because of an absence of love as a child and the history of addiction in the family. He was searching to find meaning and searching to find love, and the drugs were his surrogate. He had gotten clean in the clinic, but there was still a nagging hole he didn't know how to fill. He couldn't pinpoint what it was, but there was something deep down in his stomach, like an itch that was too deep to get to.

When Carl got to their hometown, he stopped off at a sporting goods store and bought a wooden baseball bat and then headed for his father's house.

The sight of the familiar dilapidated façade of his father's house brought tears to his eyes. Not knowing where the tears came from sent Carl into a fury, and he stormed into the house, hearing his father's loud snoring as he entered.

The police found him three hours later, curled up on his childhood bed, crying, covered in his father's blood.

"What's happened to us?" Katie tritely cried. Carl sat on the other side of the bulletproof glass with the phone pressed to his ear. He said nothing, just looked deeply into his sister's eyes.

"How is it in there?" Roger said, trying to catch his brother's attention.

"What the fuck do you care?" Carl's gaze never left Katie's.

"Don't be so mean," Katie said before a deluge of tears cascaded down her cheeks.

"Why not? He didn't come with us. He didn't help us. He just helped himself. Now he wants to know what it was like to bash that fuck's head in ..."

"That's not what I said."

"That's what you meant. You were just selfish. You went somewhere where it's legal to kill. You live in a fantasy world where nothing matters but yourself. Katie needed help. I needed help. So we helped each other."

"Yeah, getting fucked up on meth really helped us out," Roger said flatly.

"No, that was how she helped me. She got me off it. I helped her by killing that bastard."

"Please!" Katie shouted, sobbing.

"You're a fucking sociopath! How does that help her?"

"You don't understand because you weren't there. He tried to come after us. He would call and say he was coming to get us. We were paranoid, thinking he was every creak in the boards, he was every knock at the door. We started to get out, and he tried to pull us back—and you were nowhere to be found."

"I was in basic training!"

"Which you ran off to because you wouldn't help."

"You're delusional."

"You want to know what it felt like?"

"No! God, please!" Katie cried, scooting away from the glass.

"It felt liberating. With every crack of that bat I felt a little more free. After a while I wanted to feel it, so I got on my knees and punched his broken face. It was gratifying. It was *personal*."

"He left before I was even brought home from the hospital, so as far as I'm concerned I'm an immaculate conception." Sven grinned as he said it.

"He left 'cause of my mom. She was a crazy crone. Religious as shit." He stroked his St. Christopher medal as he told the story. "My sis and I went to church instead of school. We knew the Bible back and front. We even had little contests, testing to see who knew Bible verses better."

Roger rubbed down his rifle barrel with the rag, nodding along. It was the most Sven had ever said to him at once, and it was all spontaneous.

"She beat us regularly with a switch, crying and praying as she did so. It started when we were babies. I remember Gretch crying because she skinned her knee. Mother switched her until she passed out from pain. That's just how it went. We didn't know any other way."

Sven shrugged, and Roger grunted in response. He didn't want the story to end, but he didn't know how to respond.

"I killed my first cat when I was seven. I didn't mean to do it at the time. I just wanted to know how it felt to beat something. I guess I just got carried away. But there was something to it. There was something holy. Something personal. It was like our souls were interconnected for just the briefest of moments. I understood the creature. I understood what it was feeling, and at the moment of death I felt tremendous release, like my life was worth something. It was the first time I felt that. Meaning."

This time Sven grunted. He cradled his rifle in his arms like a baby as he cleaned it.

"I both caused and freed the creature from torment, and I understood what Jesus meant by accepting our sins. It was like I was projecting everything I had ever done wrong into that cat, and in the moment of death, we were both released. I held onto that cat and cried for hours, both in love and sympathy.

"I tried again and again, but I couldn't get that feeling back. I thought maybe it only happened once with every species I killed, so I tired birds and dogs and even a deer; but I never got that spiritual awakening again.

"I began to get restless. I began to feel like God had abandoned me. How could he only give me a taste of that joyous release? Then I saw my mother beat Gretch. While she was beating her, my mother kept saying something under her breath. I strained my ears, and between cracks I was shocked to hear the Lord's Prayer.

"It dawned on me that I was striving too hard for the feeling. It wasn't just the act that gave me release; it was also my state of mind. You can't really enjoy anything if you're too caught up in it. You need something to center you, something to *personalize* the matter. I needed a prayer for myself. I needed something that would give me release, something that would center me; so I used my life experience to create my own prayer."

Roger looked at him expectantly. He had heard Sven say the prayer before but had never understood its meaning. He thought about Carl killing Pete, and he wondered if Carl prayed beforehand.

"Give me cover, for every path I take leads me astray. Give me trust, for everyone I know leaves me alone. Give me love, for the care that I missed. Give me hope, for the life I will lose. Give me patience, for my regrets. Give me peace so that I may kill.

"You should use it, Rog. I see the excitement in you. I can see the dread hanging off you, the apprehension. You need something to center you, something to help you understand your place in the universe."

Roger grunted again, but inwardly he marveled at how Sven could be all at once a sociopath yet have such a deep understanding of what it meant to be human.

"I need to ask you a favor, brother, and I hate to do it this way ..." There was silence on the phone line, but Carl let it drag on. Roger knew Carl wanted him to talk first, but he didn't know what to say.

"Hello to you too, brother. How you been, Carl?" He felt sweat moisten his palm.

"Listen, I'm sorry that we've been so distant, but I know things about you. I know when you rotated back to the world you became a mercenary. I know you kept working as a sniper. I need something from you."

"Can't you at least tell me how our sister is doing? She won't talk to me either."

"Katie's fine. She lives in New York, and she works as a secretary for a high-end lawyer."

"I'm surprised you called me and not her."

"This isn't something that she needs to know about."

His tone was grave, and immediately Roger's throat went dry.

"Don't worry. You still don't have to be a part of our family, but the family needs a favor. I got into trouble."

"Listen, if this is about drugs ..."

"It is. Tomorrow you will be getting a contract for Pablo Hernandez. You need to make sure he's dead. He's the accountant for an up-and-coming cartel. He's ordered the deaths of many people, especially ones who stole from the organization. Your sister's stupid husband stole money from him, and the organization won't leave her alone until he's gone."

"The accountant doesn't matter; the documentation is what matters. The cartel will still know, and they'll go after her." Roger's hands were wet.

"Not true."

"How d'you know? Are you affiliated with them?" Roger heard Carl breathe in sharply and then sigh into the phone.

"I'm Pablo, Roger. They won't come after her because I'll get rid of the records. But when I do that, they're going to come after me, and the things they would do … they'd make me tell them who owed the money. This is the best way."

Roger didn't answer right away.

"You're asking me to kill you? Are you serious?"

"Don't get fucking righteous on me now. You're the one who ran. You're the one who stayed away. You're the one who stays alone. You're the killer. We all inherited something from our fuck-up of a father. I inherited his foul temper and addictions, Katie inherited his tenacity, and you inherited the selfishness. I will never forgive you for running out on us like our mother, but you can do this one thing for us. I expect you to be responsible for once in your life. Katie will die without your help."

"I can't do that." There was no conviction in his voice. The shock was too much, and under a veil of confidence there was a layer of fear eating away at him. His life had finally caught up to him. He had run to forget his childhood. He had run for a new beginning. He had run in the hope that he could forget who he was, but he'd come to realize that Sven was right. You need to embrace who you are. You need to understand your place in the universe.

"You'd better fucking do it. I've tried killing myself, but I can't bring myself to it. This is your retribution; this is what you were meant to do. I'm prepared. You'd better fucking do it."

You must accept your place in the universe. "Carl ..." *You need something to center you.* "... if you need me, you know I'm there."

"That's what I thought."

Carl stood smiling in the center of his crosshairs. Roger took a deep breath and settled his finger on the trigger one more time. He thought it ironic that he had been so much closer to Sven than he ever was to his own brother. He thought about the juxtaposition between what his brother had told him on the phone and what Sven had told him while describing his life: *This is what you were meant to do. You must accept your place in the universe.*

The prayer started to emit from his lips without him realizing it.

"Give me cover, for every path I take leads me astray." Carl turned back to the buyer, and Roger felt relief rush over him, knowing he wouldn't have to look Carl in the face.

"Give me trust, for everyone I know leaves me alone." His sister was married, and he hadn't even known about it. Carl was an accountant for a cartel, and he didn't know about it.

"Give me love, for the care that I missed." His father had been killed by his son for past abuses. Killed to accept the sins of the sons. Killed to absolve future wrongs.

"Give me hope, for the life I will lose." That human feeling of expectation. That feeling that Sven knew so well. The life that you start to win or start to lose from the moment you are born.

"Give me patience, for my regrets." Leaving when he did and coming back the *way* he did.

"Give me peace so that I may kill." His finger slowly squeezed, and the recoil conveyed the gravity of the situation. Through the scope he saw Carl fall. The woman ran for cover.

Roger quickly packed his materials, marveling at the simplicity of the act and the peace he felt. There was something terribly personal about his act. He had felt connected with his brother as he squeezed the trigger. He felt as though their spirits had briefly touched, and he felt gratitude and pride. Suddenly he understood what Sven had been talking about during his story about the cat— that feeling, as though this was meant to happen. This is what he was meant to do. He had saved his remaining family and found his place in the universe. His brothers helped him find the way.

Déjà Vu

"I had a dream about this room." I look about the room, but despite the intimate knowledge I have of it and its inhabitant, I feel odd here. There's something off about the room, cold ambivalence, amplified by the empty stare of the psychiatrist. I'd hoped mentioning the dream might elicit more of a response from the doctor, but all I get is an indifferent nod. Par for the course.

"You," I say, waggling a finger at him, "were not in the room." I look up at the psychiatrist expectantly, but the doctor is lost in his notebook. I feel a flash of anger, imagining a notebook full of doodles of women with big breasts on far-off islands.

"It was all empty." I decide that if the doctor is indeed doing this, at least he's got a pair of ears. He's something to talk *at*, if not necessarily to. Relief abounds through disclosure, even if no one's listening.

"Only the couch where I'm sitting and the picture on

the wall." I raise my hand and point at a reproduction of *The Scream* on the wall. I often muse over its presence, how indicative it is of a psychiatric office to have a painting so disconnected from reality, with a person lost in dark colors, screaming, holding his head in torment, perceiving a future horror. It's something so ingrained in popular culture that you don't even have to be a connoisseur of art to recognize it. I think, however, the juxtaposition of fantasy and reality, caught so conclusively in the painting, is lost to most—maybe even to the doctor.

"Does that make sense? That painting in my dream? Why would I be here, in this room, instead of in my own? Or in the park? And why would there be only this couch and that painting? Is my subconscious trying to tell me something? Am I unhappy with my life and is the screamer supposed to indicate that I need change? Is that how I feel subconsciously?"

I lean back on the couch as I talk, almost forgetting the doctor is sitting across from me. In fact I can't imagine stopping. I'm on a roll, monologuing my problems out. But when I pause to begin a new direction, something about women, about loneliness, the doctor clears his throat.

I snap my head up to query the doctor. Not a word is spoken, but enough has been said. Time is up, and the doctor will hear no more.

"You know, you could be a little more cordial when I come here. I spend a lot of money on you, and all you can do is point at a watch or clear your throat." I again look expectantly at the doctor, who says nothing, just crosses his legs and smiles pedantically.

"Fair enough. Same time next week, I hope? If I'm not boring you too much?"

I chuckle as I walk out of the office. I knew the doctor wouldn't respond, but it was the kind of therapy I was looking for. I'm not sure if I could actually handle someone trying to analyze me. Silence seems to work best for me, and somehow the doctor knows this.

I've been going there for over a year, long enough to wonder if the doctor can even form a coherent phrase. Before starting therapy, I had felt tired and worn down, like someone was taking a nail file to my soul. I'd wake up in the morning and go through the motions, gather my paychecks, and pay off each month's rent. Dire times for the uncertain.

My entire life I've dreamt of other places. A daydreamer by nature, retail grunt by trade. What could be greater, I think, than for a disaster to happen in the world? Something catastrophic. A cacophony of whining birds, screaming metal, and moaning people. That'd be a place where I wouldn't have to worry about progress reports and being seven minutes late for work, ducking the boss. That would be a place where I could be a hero. I could lead.

I look around the intersection when I get to the bottom of the staircase. It amazes me that a psychiatry practice would be atop a Hawaiian barbeque restaurant, but I swear by the results. Since coming here I've felt less pressure, less stressed; my mind feels more at ease these days.

Busy intersection. I feel a slight waft of ocean air, crisp breeze with a modicum of brine thrown in for good measure. The minimal amount of smog always amazed me, living in a city like this; the ocean air transports the chemicals across the bay. That breeze does wonders.

I live three blocks away from my shrink's office, another reason why it's so easy to come here. Proximity makes the world go 'round, but often I feel a longing to be farther off. It appeals to my dreamy nature. Dreamers are always travelers, just not necessarily doers.

Ambling down the few blocks to my house is always an adventure. There are four homeless men who live on my block. Two of them, however, prefer to be called bums; the difference is miniscule to most people, but the two hint periodically that they have an apartment together.

I laughed out loud the first time they told me this. I'd been giving the two of them—a tall, angular black man named Red and a smaller, emaciated vet named Milton—money for years. When I found out they not only had jobs but that they actually had an apartment together, I was shocked. Well, almost. It takes a lot to be shocked in this city.

Red and Milton are an original odd couple. I often wonder what social gatherings would be like at their apartment, everyone panhandling the next person to walk in the door. If you're fashionably late, you're broke.

The third bum is a much more annoying individual. Scary Larry, the locals call him. He's an old, short, white pederast who blames the world for his psychosis. I often marvel when I see Larry walking down the street in a beat-up old suit, as if he is attending a spellbinding rendition of *Cabaret* at the trash can on the left.

The fourth is a much more sinister character who wanders around aimlessly wearing a beanie down over his eyes and baggy clothes that swallow his waifish body. He's known to walk the streets and follow women. There's even a rumor that he attacked a woman in her own kitchen. Spooky, this cast of characters, but it's all part of the area's charm. Serious, yet playful; sophisticated, yet naïve.

This is my world. This is the place I call home, this neighborhood with its fascinating inhabitants. However I have a place much more sacred to me than any place I've called home, a place just as significant as the doctor and the sanity he lends me. A park. They call it "the Skinny" for short, but its real name is Tamskinelli Park. It's a quiet park that people don't frequent; they just pass through. It's the kind of park where you can be alone with your thoughts. It's a wonderful place to gain perspective.

Dusk descends upon my neighborhood, placing a crimson glow on the small mom-and-pop businesses. Relief washes over me as I take a deep breath, stuff my hands into my pockets, and saunter down the three blocks, knowing my issues have been left to float around my psychiatrist's office. It's a comfortable feeling. I know my surroundings, the buildings, the people. I stroll like a man with no cares, pushing everything to the back of my mind. I'm done with work, and I don't have another shift for fifty-four hours. I have no other obligations for the evening. It's just me alone with my thoughts.

When I get to my corner I see Red and Milton hanging out in front of my doorstep. A small smile creeps across my face; these two are always a riot.

"Fuckin' lady!" Milton spits out. "Bitch don't know what's good for her. All I did was go up there and ask her for change!" He took a step back and sat down in his rusted old wheelchair, which was covered in bumper stickers. I always wondered why Milton went to the trouble of putting those things on there. They don't seem to make any rational kind of sense. "Baby on Board" is plastered next to "Honk if You're Horny." (That one always tickled me. Milton cornered me on more than one occasion and proceeded to tell me how much he *loved* pussy.) And who could forget the ever popular "I EAT SHIT" in big bold letters by the right wheel?

"Whoa, man, cool it. Be cool, man. She's just a lady!" Red is eloquent in his way. His lower jaw juts out at you when he talks as if he's constantly tying to catch an afternoon drizzle.

"Fucking bitch. I wheeled up to her and was like 'Hey, got any change, babe?' and she turned on me like an eagle and was like"—Milton raises the pitch of his voice and, strangely enough, does indeed sound like a scorned woman—"'You lazy, lazy man! I saw you walking around. There is nothing wrong with your leg!'"

I descend the block to where they are and raise my eyebrows, inviting conversation. Milton has eyes that burrow into you. He looks through you rather than at you. Everything is intense with Milton, even if you're only talking. He has a way of looking at you, as if he is imploring you to like him, which in turn makes it hard not to. But there are times when the anger boils over in his system and he looks like a ravaged tiger ready to spring. As small as he is, he doesn't seem like a problem; but if you look into his eyes, a blue and red fusion of hate and anguish, you'll feel his pain, and it's impossible for you to turn away.

"What you say to her, man?" Red sounded as if he was both very drunk and stoned at the same time. His cadence was slow and rhythmic, and his physiognomy was that of a retarded twelve-year-old boy. He was, however, as sharp as a knife.

"I says to her, I says, 'Fuck you, lady!' Then I showed her." Milton grabbed his pant leg and slowly lifted it as if both Red and I had never before seen the grotesque. His shin actually looked as if someone had made a bowl out of it. Three inches deep. It's a wonder he can stand at all.

"And she screamed and went running off, the bitch. I tell ya, people are fucking stupid. The bitch, no idea what the fuck she's saying, the bitch."

Red chimes in with his phlegmatic wisdom. "Here, man, have a cigarette." His jaw juts out, bottom teeth showing, but he has the most caring eyes a person could ever see.

I smile down at Milton and Red. The world is right today. I feel at ease, no more tension in my shoulders.

I tap Red on the shoulder and move past without saying anything.

I hear Red's voice behind me. "Hey, man, you got any cigarettes?"

I turn around and look directly at the cigarettes he has already brought out for Milton's consumption. Red follows my gaze and smiles.

"You know," Red says with a chuckle, "one for the road."

"One for the road, right," I say and pop a cigarette out for Red. I pause and then give him two. "One for the road."

"Hey, all right, man! Take it easy!" Red takes what I like to call Red's jazz pose: right hand outstretched and right foot extended and upturned.

"Night, guys," I say as I enter my building.

Nights are always the worst—nothing to do but think about what you've done during the day, who you've loved, and who you've hated. Night could be a wonderful time if I was happy, but it *isn't* a wonderful time for me. Downtime creates residual restlessness.

I fancy myself an insomniac, although clinically, I am probably no more than a poor sleeper. I don't go nights without sleeping; it just takes a long time for sleep to take over. It doesn't matter the bed or the pillow; it doesn't matter what comforter. Sleep is always just a long time coming.

I think of many things while trying to sleep. I think of girls and friends. I fantasize about being a hero and saving some baby from a burning building. I dream about being a famous writer and traveling the globe, writing my world-famous books. I do this while staring at a spider that has made my ceiling his roost. I ignore the dust that carpets my room and the webs that encrust my walls. No point in dwelling on the present when you can be wishing for a future.

I sigh and scan the books lined up against my walls, wondering what to read today. I search through my endless library and decide that tonight I don't have much of an attention span. I settle on a short story collection, *Cthulhu and Other Oddities*. I've always had a fancy for the fantastic. Otherworldly things appeal to my dreamer's nature. I lay down, taking note that for tonight, thank God, there will be no setting of the alarm clock. I have that freedom.

The book cracks open, and my eyes scan across the title of the first story, "The Yellow Wallpaper." I read it, though I don't really understand it. I'm not sure whether I fall asleep as I read or if the story is just *that* disjointed.

My dreams are enigmatic—short, jolty scenes where aberrant images clash. I see the park, or rather the area of the park I frequent. There's a lush, almost swamp-like pond, complete with a fallen tree trunk carved into a bench; it's a perfect place to write, nothing but all the time in the world to create.

In the dream, though, this scene isn't the serene venue

that I want it to be. The water is like pitch, motionless and menacing. There is a breeze in the air, usually indicative of an ocean zephyr. I glance up at the sky, expecting the usual opaque navy, but instead it's scarlet.

I want to keep looking, intrigued by the oddity, wanting to know more, but instead my head whips down to see someone crawling out of the brackish water. It's a tall man who seems to be impervious to water. It rolls off him as if he is a *duck*. He's wearing a red beanie and a black trench coat. I immediately recognize him and thank God I'm not a woman in my kitchen. Strangely, I seem to understand what's happening so lucidly. I wonder how it could be a dream.

He crawls, jerking, up the incline toward me and raises his head. The beanie is pulled down over his face, but I can see his mouth, teeth big enough to split both lips. I slap my hands to my face and scream. The world fades, and lines streak like running paint. I feel wallpaper underneath my fingernails.

I sit up in my bed, and the book falls to the floor with a thump. I resolve to stop eating spicy food before bed.

In the morning I decided I must face my fears and my dream. I must go to my spot and contemplate.

The day is windy and gray. My breath burns in my lungs, a cold burn, as I pump my legs, pedaling my bike to reach my destination. I feel despondent about my lack of exercise. This shouldn't be nearly as hard as it is.

Every time I see the park I'm amazed. It seems to have a glow about it that separates it from the downtrodden, cobbled neighborhood. It has a resplendent warmth, a golden aura. Just being able to see the park puts me more at ease.

I lay my bike down in the grass and trudge to my destination, weary of the conjured creatures of my mind. Obviously I'm being paranoid, right? Dreams are just dreams, but reality has a terrifying thinness to it, the cold makes me embrace the lucidity of my surroundings. No, if this were a dream I wouldn't be cognizant of the burn in my lungs, which has not yet receded.

The pond has a light green tint to it, and the tree-bark bench has a soft, worn feel to it. I stare down at the spot where the creature ascended in my dream. Today it is a frog, nothing more.

I see strange things sometimes. Solid objects wave, like air rippling across water. I mention this now because it's what the dirt is doing. Previously I have told people of this oddity, thinking it wasn't abnormal. All people must get this from time to time. Apparently this is not the case. I have been accused of being a burnout. Too much acid, people say, but that isn't the truth. I've never done drugs. My perception is too vapid to even try them for fear of that quality deepening.

I pull my gaze away from the quivering dirt and cast my eyes toward the houses in the distance. Business as usual. After a moment, a car passes. Pause. A car passes. Pause. A car passes. People are doing their daily thing, furiously and frivolously going from point to point.

The only divergence I see is through my peripheral

vision: a man standing in the shadows of an oak at the perimeter of the park. His hand is resting on the fallen trunk, and he seems to be looking at me. I try to get a better look at him, but when I peer closer he's gone. A shadow person.

This is another thing that happens to me periodically. They pop out of the corners of my vision, as if I'm lonely and my subconscious is creating partners for me to commune with. They're hardly ever there, but when they are, I startle them much more than they startle me. I have scared many an elderly lady. Still wondering about the drugs?

Goddamn, it's time to see the doctor again.

I pounce up the stairs and reach his door. Closed and locked. Damn. I stand there for a minute and wonder what good it will do to knock. Chances are he isn't here. After all, I don't actually have an appointment. I've come unannounced before, but I guess it'll have to be another day.

Red and Milton are standing in front of my door again. Déjà vu. Routines facilitate memory. It is far easier to remember what you did yesterday if it happens every day. This is my curse. I try as hard as I can to avoid the mainstream. I work because I have to, but small talk doesn't ease the mind, it collapses it. Right?

Milton seems better today; he has a big grin on his face, his cheeks wrinkling up around his eyes. I don't think I can bear talking to these two again today. I feel dizzy, probably from riding my bike uphill on the way to the park, but even though a while has passed since then, I still don't feel good.

I jump off the bike and walk it over past the two vagrants to my house. They notice me but seem involved in some kind of conversation as I pass. I turn and wave. This is a mistake.

I run right into someone, square into his chest, and though he has a small frame, he doesn't move. I turn my head with an apology on my lips, and I see Larry. The crazy asshole. And now he has something to yell at me for. Shit.

"You see 'em, too? I seen 'em on the corner! They *sneaky*. They *hard*. They haunt! They always there, ain't they? Just 'round the corner! Waitin' fer ya! They'll get ya." His eyes are on fire; normally gray, they are now sunsets; the waving bright colors flow like water. His mind is gone.

I was expecting him to scream bloody murder at me. I was expecting to feel a barrage of fists. But, no, I get Larry with an eager face, wanton, imploring. It scares me.

"Goddamn it, you need to sleep more." The same thing I tell myself. "They're only your imagination, bad food, and sleep deprivation." The same thing I tell myself.

"Naïve, boy! They comin' for ya." I don't see humanity in his eyes anymore. I'm not sure if I ever did; but all I see now is a wall. I see bricks that he has laid throughout the years adding to this persona. The façade has become real. Larry, as he was—whatever he was—is no more. He is behind that wall. This is what remains. I imagine this is what happens to people when they go crazy; they put themselves behind a wall to protect themselves.

"Good for them." I hear the disdain in my voice. I hear the anger. It's not really anger at him, though. It's his mannerisms. They terrify me. They have the swagger of a man who seems to have something so heavy on his conscious that it drags him down into a hunch. His big, waving arm gestures punctuate his statements and terrify me. They remind me of me.

I slip past Larry, ignoring the imploring shells that were once his eyes. I glance back at Red and Milton. They are both looking at me—not at the pair of us, Larry and I, not at the little squabble that we have just had—but at me. Red lifts his head a little and whispers something to me. I think I understand the concern in his face and the darkness of his eyes. His broken lips mouth, "Be careful."

Too much. I've had too much. I have to go inside. I'm getting loopy, dizzy. I need to sleep. I slam through the doorway and take the steps two at a time, my bike forgotten in the hallway. Forget the bike. Two at a time. I gotta get to sleep. I feel even worse. Everything is spinning. Two at a time. Can I take three? It's getting dark. Two at a time. The front door seems *so far away*. Two at a time. Two at a time. Two at a time. Door. Room. Bed. Sleep. Déjà vu.

I wake to find that I haven't slept at all. I feel like I've run a marathon. I am exhausted, lying in bed, watching the shadows of a nearby tree snake across my ceiling. I need air; I'm being suffocated. A thick haze covers the room. I've woken in a cloud.

I feel dizzy and out of sorts. Everything around me almost seems like it might be a dream, as if I'm sleeping right now. But I can feel the pins and needles in my right calf, that slow and warm crawl back and forth, sporadic patterns lacing my legs. I need a walk. I'm sure fresh air will clear my head. It's too muggy in this apartment. It doesn't lull you to sleep; it suffocates you.

I sit and collect my thoughts, with my head in my hands. I can't do it. I feel crazy, shaken, buzzed, except I am cognizant of my actions. I stand, swaying and rubbing my forehead as I make my way toward the door. I feel slimy, greasy, as if I am coated in a sheen of Crisco. The more I wipe, the dirtier I seem to get. I can't believe I'm walking outside like this.

Outside, I near the park. The air helps. I feel a bit sharper. I know I can never go back inside; I couldn't stand the claustrophobia. My tight lungs stretch desperately, trying to get air. A burning sensation.

There are shades here, shadow people peering from behind trees, Outlines. Shapes. If I were alone on the road I would be scared, but with people here, I know that they'll stay where they are—at the edges. Irrational thoughts, for sure. But what would you think if you saw people at the edge of your vision? So what if you knew they weren't real? What if they *were* real?

There is so much clean air in the woods. I think maybe I could take a nap out here. I must be tired. That's why the shadow people are coming out. That's why they're creeping so close. I thought I had slept. Did I sleep? Did I dream the whole thing? I thought I slept. Maybe it was a daydream. How sad … daydreaming about dreaming.

I can breathe out here. Clean air, full of oxygen, moving the toxins out.

I *need* to go to the doctor.

They pump oxygen into casinos to keep people awake, keep their senses clear so they can gamble longer. I can't sleep out here.

A shadow person just ran across the field ahead. Am I dreaming? Wait, where did everyone go?

There's another one.

I thought people were around. Oh, I'm dizzy. Another one.

Am I dreaming? Or are they real? Another one.

It's getting dark. No, my eyes closed. Another one. Maybe the fresh air is working.

Very dark.

I wake into a dream. I'm still in the park. No shadow people around now. Is it a dream? I just lay down. Feels like a dream. Feels warm. The park at night is not warm. I must be sleeping! The walk worked.

"Ya must run now. It won't take 'em long. They's found ya tonight. Ya best be careful." The words are coming from behind me.

I turn and bump into Larry. He is standing in front of me, close. He smiles at me, winking. Oh, it's getting dark again. Or ...

No, my eyes were closed. I'm still in the park. I feel agoraphobic. I have to get inside.

I need to see the doctor.

Déjà vu.

In the street I see a man. He looks angry.

"Psychotic punk! Did you think you could get away with it?"

Is he talking to me? He isn't looking at me.

"Pull that wallet out! I know you have a knife! Where's the gun?"

He grabs my hands and pulls them to his chest. *What the hell?*

"You fucked my wife! Drug addict! Pilferer!"

Why won't he let go of me?

"Let go of me!"

He looks *crazy*.

"You're holding on to me!"

I'm very confused.

"Leave me *alone*!"

He screams like a woman.

I let go, and he runs away. I shake my hands and ... it's getting dark. Again.

I wake on the street. I'm clothed and walking. I'm not wearing the same thing I was before. Different clothes, different day, I guess. I see Red and Milton in front of my house.

Milton seems better today; he has a big grin on his face, his cheeks wrinkling up around his eyes. I don't think I can bear talking to these two again today. I feel dizzy, probably from riding my bike uphill on the way to the park, but even though a while has passed since then, I still don't feel good.

Wait, did I ride my bike today?

I'm *dizzy*.

I see the guy from my dream in the distance. He's wearing different clothes too. Different clothes, different day. It's a gray hoodie with a black beanie this time. He's following a girl too. I take a step toward them, and I see Red out of the corner of my eye. He's trying to tell me something. I squint my eyes. He mouths, "Be careful." I frown and look back toward the guy from my dreams.

He's close to the girl now. He's walking fast, and she looks worried. I try to move toward them, but I'm *dizzy*. I see her reach into her pockets, reaching for keys, I presume. *Get the keys.* He pulls his hands out of his pockets. *Get the keys.* His nails are long, ugly. Dirty. *Get the keys.* What is she waiting for? *Get the keys!* It's getting so dark. *GET THE KEYS!* He's a *demon*! Grab. The. *Keys*!

Too slow. He takes her. Jumps over her shoulders. Nails digging into her shoulders. Those teeth. Big enough to split both lips. They bite, tearing and ripping. She screams. She never got the keys. It's so dark. I see people walking toward me through the darkness. Shadow people, I know. I can see them clearly. A hand on my shoulder. I turn and see Red standing there. He looks sad, but I'm so dizzy. A hand on my shoulder. I turn and see Red standing there. He looks sad, but I'm so dizzy. A hand on my shoulder. I turn and see Red standing there. He looks sad, but I'm so dizzy. A hand on my shoulder. "Be careful." Déjà vu.

I find myself in the doctor's office. It's cold. I think one of the windows is broken. What day is it?

"What day is it?" He looks at me and shakes his head. I think of the park. The Skinny they call it. The *Skin*-ny. There is a glow there. It's a glow of gold. It feels good there. Feels *thin*. "Why am I here today? Did you agree to meet me?"

The doctor shrugs his shoulders and shakes his head. He's skinny. He's thin. He seems familiar. Déjà vu.

"Why the scream? Am I screaming?" The painting. Paint. Scream.

His hands go to his face. Screaming. *Thin*. He's paint. He's running. The paint, *leaking*. The room is bare. No scream, no doctor. Why am I here? I need the park. It's getting so dark. All the time. Must be winter. When do I work? Friday. I like Friday. It's skinny. Oh yeah, the park.

It's cold here. I can only see through a pinhole. Shadow people blur my vision. They're so close. Do I have keys? I NEED TO GRAB MY KEYS! Déjà vu.

I rip the doctor off the wall. The *painting*. The *Scream* off the wall. It's too much. How could you put that in a doctor's office? I feel something under my fingernails. Yellow wallpaper. Déjà vu.

The pond. I look to my pond. It's *so cold*. I look in my pond. I see myself crawling out of it. Déjà vu. I wear a red beanie, and my teeth split my lips. I crawl *into* it. The pond is *skinny*. I reach the bottom fast.

The bottom is the doctor's office. I see the scream on the wall. The doctor is too. Screaming. It's so dark. Déjà vu.

Larry enters the room with a wide-eyed expectancy. He is being followed by a shadow person. He feels the shadow person pulling at his brain, stretching his sanity like taffy. The room is cold and dark. Soap covers the windows.

The room is bare, nothing covering the walls, not even wallpaper, only a dingy, brown mold. The hardwood floors are pulled up at points, leaving small protrusions that are perfect for stubbing a toe.

A stiff breeze flies into the room, and Larry shivers when he sees the man lying in the corner. He is curled up into a ball with a red pool surrounding him. The window is smashed in; glass is sprayed everywhere. The man has a piece of glass grasped firmly in his right hand. Larry takes note that his fingernails are either bent back or torn off, as if he has been digging in the walls.

Larry shakes his head and turns back to the door. He sees the gouges in the wall next to the door; they are deep, and some are splattered with blood.

Larry respects the man. He saw the shadow people; he ran from the shadow people, and then he stood up to them. He fought back.

People around the neighborhood call him Scary Larry. People think he's crazy. They're afraid of him. But there's something that the people around the neighborhood don't know about, something they would be much more scared about.

The shadow people.

They came from the park. They took this man. They've been coming for Larry for years. He just knows how to run. He moves past the gouges in the walls and out the door to the old office. It amazes him that no one ever saw the man going up the stairs. Maybe they did. Maybe they didn't care. Maybe they thought he was crazy. Just another bum.

Larry reaches the bottom of the staircase and sees light traffic at the intersection. Out of the corner of his eye, he sees two shadow people, one on his right and one on the left. Time to run.

THE DREAM

"Don't worry about it, son," Justin's father said. "Some people like to believe these dreams are a premonition of events in a person's life. This, however, seems to be just a single, ordinary, garden-variety nightmare. People have this type of dream all the time. All it means is you've been sitting in front of the TV for too long or you spent too much time playing on the computer. It'll eventually go away. All you have to do is try and ignore it. Try and wake yourself up while when you have 'em, and they should fade out."

"But every time I have one of these, I die. It's really starting to freak me out, Dad! Especially 'cause it keeps coming back."

"Think very hard now, son. At the end of the dream, do you really die? You may think you do, but if the dream cuts short right before anything happens to you, you should be okay."

"Well, I guess I never really die in it. It's just that it is really startin' to scare me. I've had this stupid dream for five days in a row, and I don't want to deal with it anymore."

"It'll go away. Don't worry about that. If it doesn't, we can always take you to the clinic, and they'll process the dreams and tell us what the underlying message is. But you've got to be careful about one thing: if you keep having this dream, right at the point where you're captured and you fear death, do whatever you can—*but don't die.*"

"Why? What's the big deal?"

"If you are in a situation where you die in your dream, that means that in real life you'll die." His father sat back smugly, offering a small, almost imperceptible smirk.

It was back, the terrible dream that'd been haunting him the past few nights. It started out innocently enough. He was hiking on the trail behind his house, no big deal. But, though it was just a flat, short trail, he felt tired as he careened through the twists and turns. Everywhere he turned he saw birds lying dead on the ground, an omen of the events yet to occur. He could see his house in the distance, and he could tell something was wrong. The house had been tainted somehow. There was some angle that was different, or maybe some brick was laid wrong; something about the house just wasn't right. But still he moved toward it, getting to the edge of the woods, passing the brick fireplace, and entering his backyard.

With each step, fatigue grew in his muscles even though he was clearly in a dream. His vision got blurry around the periphery, making it seem like one of those cheesy flashbacks he had seen so often in the movies.

Despite the knowledge that he was in the middle of a dream, the fireplace still scared him. Even now, when he was almost seventeen, the fireplace haunted his thoughts. He knew there was nothing there, nothing that could hurt him. It was just something the previous owner had thought would improve the house's looks, but he still couldn't shake the feeling. On top of that, the dream seemed to deepen his neuroses regarding the brick structure. He looked at it and couldn't help but think that it was some remnant of an ancient house that had burned to the ground, something from the Civil War-era, with the ghosts of soldiers haunting it, bound by some unbelievable desire to right past wrongs.

In his waking moments, he had always given it a wide berth when passing it, but in the dream, he wanted to go toward it. He wanted to see what was in it, what it was made of, what was burnt in it. It was an antique, not meant for human contact.

But what if there was something from the previous owners in the ashes of the fire? What if there were clues about the inhabitants still hanging around this place? He could be the one to find out. He could be the big hero. The headlines would show his picture under a headline like "Local Boy Uncovers Mystery of Lost Soldier."

He walked up to it, feeling the absolute *strangeness*

in the atmosphere. Something about the fireplace was wrong. He was getting the same feeling that he got from the house; something was wrong with it. But still he continued to move slowly along the small brick wall toward the deadly quiet fireplace.

There was some kind of vibe coming from it, as if it were a natural fan, gently blowing air away from it and warning him to turn back before it was too late. He had come too far, though. Curiosity killed the cat, they say; apparently it could kill seventeen-year-olds too. He reached the hearth and put his hand into the ashes. He could see them sifting around his fingers, but he couldn't feel them. It was as though they were made of air.

Then he realized what was wrong with the fireplace and house. They weren't real. They had an aura of transparency, even though he couldn't see through them.

Then the fog around his peripheral vision tightened, and the whole world seemed to shift. They *were* transparent. He *could* see through them. He could make out the basic features of his surroundings, but there was something dramatically different. They were surrounded by a blackness that seemed to be quickly spreading, dissolving the world. He felt his heart drop as he remembered what was about to happen next.

The ground and his surroundings disappeared, leaving him to free fall through the darkness. All he could see was the blackness of space. He was falling through the void. He had experienced this same feeling many times, whether he was in school during one of his boring lectures, or just when he was lying on his bed watching TV, buzzing in and out of reality. It was a familiar feeling, and every time it happened, he jerked himself awake. He had even done this in English class, when their sexist teacher was lecturing about how Mary Shelley had not actually written *Frankenstein* but that her husband, Percy Shelley, had. He had never totally understood the sexism; but it wasn't a subject he cared about, so he just shut down to get another half hour of sleep. When he had started to dream fall again, he jerked himself right out of his desk.

This dream, however, was completely different. He could make himself jerk around, but he could never wake. He even knew he was dreaming, but when he tried to wake himself he just kept falling.

He just fell and fell and fell. After some time, the blackness around him began to clear, and he could see he was in trouble. He was falling into his backyard, only about thirty yards from the fireplace. He could see the house, as normal as ever, and he could see the old brick fireplace was normal as well; but he still felt apprehension. There was something menacing about its visage. He kept falling, and as he looked down, he saw that he was going to land in the pool.

Every time he'd had this dream, he had flown down into the pool at what seemed faster than terminal velocity, which sent him into depths deeper than the pool was capable of holding. He wasn't just falling into the pool; he was sinking into the earth.

When he finally stopped, he tried to break the water's

surface, but everything was black. He was back in the void, suffocating as it gently held him. This world was struggling to be created, not struggling to stay alive.

He swam and swam, not sure if he was going in the right direction; but as always, he made his way to the top. He felt panic seep into his heart and brain, eaten from the inside by the fear he might not make it out of the dream alive. Then, just before he lost hope and gave up to sink back down into the void, he breached the surface … just as he always did.

He reached up for the wall of the pool and pulled himself out. The blur came back, covering the outside corners of his field of vision. But more powerful than anything was the pull of the brick fireplace.

He distinctly knew he wouldn't fall through it like he just had. He was on a lower level of hell; there would be something worse. He walked to the brick structure, feeling no fear, as if the events he knew were about to transpire didn't affect his thought process, as if he thought he were just out for an innocent walk.

The fatigue imposed itself again, making it hard for him to reach his destination. His body was trying to tell him something. There was danger up ahead, and he knew it. But his brain didn't seem to want to listen. He pushed himself through the pain, sure he could get there, certain that he could uncover the mysteries that lay in that forlorn structure.

When he finally made it, he collapsed, sending ash from past fires into the air. He looked at them, thinking about their beauty as they flew against the backdrop of the dusk sky. They were the lords of all creation; they could do whatever they wanted. They planned out their lives, their futures, and their pasts. It was amazing how so much beauty could come out of destruction.

He made the effort to roll over onto his stomach so he could look into the fireplace, to hold the ash and the burnt wood, to hold that destruction. He felt himself begin to cry for no reason. He knew it would happen, but he had no control over it. It really was quite silly, to cry over burnt wood and ashes, but at that moment it was as if he could feel the pain the wood had felt as it burned. Laying there, unable to move, as someone doused you in lighter fluid. Watching them strike a match and throw it on you. Feeling the flames burn through the fluid and catch a hold of you.

He shuddered, feeling goose bumps spread over his arms. He rolled over, unable to look on the destruction in the fireplace, and instead watched the bits of ash floating in the air. They all seemed so happy despite their horrible births. He steadied his gaze on the largest as it floated down into reach. He reached up for it and felt its silky texture, but as soon as he grabbed it, something grabbed him.

The tears immediately stopped flowing, and his hair stood on end. He looked down to see another hand grasping at him, coming up from the ground. He immediately jumped up, despite his aching muscles, yanking at the hand, which still gripped him. In doing so, he pulled an arm out of the ashes. The skin attached to it was rotten and flaking away, leaving mostly dirty bone. He tried to pull back, but all he succeeded in doing was pulling the arm out to the shoulder.

He changed tactics and worked on the fingers instead, peeling them off one by one, but he wasn't strong enough to hold them. Each one he pulled off latched back onto him, holding him in a death grip, as he tried to pry the next finger off. He backed away again, forcing a head to pop out of the ground. The head was rotten just like the hand and the arm, leaving mostly flaking skin and a grim, smiling skull.

The rest of the body arose on its own. Another hand shot through the ground, grabbing his leg and pulling him off balance. As he tumbled to the ground, he saw the thing pull up. It seemed to be a zombie, but it was nothing like the walking dead from legends. They had most of their skin. They seemed like normal people in a trance. This was much different. The creature's garb was a Union Army uniform from the Civil War. The stink on its breath was almost unbearable, like that of his father when he was drinking, and the teeth chattered together. The animated corpse crawled toward him.

He was too tired to get up off of the ground though, so he just lay there and waited for his fate, waited for the creature to do him in. To kill him.

When the zombie reached him, it slowly slid its bony hands around his neck and began to squeeze. This was when he always woke up, with the stench of death in his nostrils.

"It happened again last night."

"What did?"

"The dream that I was telling you about! It happened again! The zombie got out of the ground crawled over and started to strangle me. I could feel the air cutting off! There has to be something I can do to stop this. I'm afraid to go to sleep at night because every time I have the dream I feel closer to death! I don't want to die like this! I'm only seventeen years old!"

"There's nothing that can really be done for dreams, son. I'm sorry, but I don't know what to tell you. I lied to you before, though; you can't actually die from dying in your dreams. I was just trying to scare you a bit, and I guess I went a little overboard. You have nothing to worry about. The next time that you have this dream ..."

"Tonight! The next time will be tonight!"

"Tonight, then. The next time that you have this dream, let it span out. I didn't mean to scare you as much as I did, but the past is gone. So let it finish. Try to stay asleep, and you'll see that you'll get away from the thing."

"Zombie."

"Zombie. You'll get away from the zombie, and you'll probably even beat the thing to a pulp. Dreams are the place you can be a hero. Where you save the day and come out all right. Even nightmares have their soft side. Think about it, no matter how bad they get, something good always happens. Or even if everyone else gets hurt or dies, in *your* nightmare *you* always come out all right.

Whatever's going on inside of your head just let it flow out. Don't stop it. That way you can let it play out, and hopefully tomorrow it'll be gone."

Justin's father took another drink.

Things never turn out how they're supposed to. The dream proceeded with the unnatural slowness, running its course. The same events took place, in the same order, with the same lucidity. The zombie had a hold of his throat. The stench of death crept in around him. He felt the evil invade his skin as the bony hands squeezed and squeezed his life out of his body. He felt like this was the last thing he'd see, this fireplace and the dying embers floating around him in the stillness of the night air. This zombie was going to take his life and take from him everything that was so beautiful in this place. Justin suddenly got angry and reached up to grab onto the zombies old decayed hands. He pulled with all of his might … to no avail. The thing still held tight to his neck. The thing still *squeezed* his neck. He couldn't stop it. The hope he held a second earlier was gone, and he could smell death and vodka as it permeated his lungs. No air could get in, just that smell, the impending destruction of his human form. Tears fell from his eyes as the world around him slowly slipped into blackness.

"Help, please," he said in a little voice. "Don't." He got this out more assertively. He somehow managed to look back into the gaping eyeholes of the monster that was slowly taking his life for its own. He saw the grin on its face, the thinning hair falling over its face as it applied more force, squeezing his neck more tightly.

"I'm sorry," it said to him. "I didn't mean to do this." He could hear the sorrow in the monster's voice, the pain it was experiencing. But the monster was still grinning.

"This was the only way it could be. You must understand, Justin," it continued. The grin widened, and the grip faltered for a second. It was enough for Justin to get one breath of fresh air. With that one breath he felt his life and hope return.

The zombie gripped down hard again, settling into the bruises on his neck.

"You just aren't as good as me," the zombie whispered into his ear. "I just can't let you carry on my name."

Justin looked back into the zombie's face, and for the first time noticed it had deep blue eyes. Those eyes penetrated his own, torturing him, for he knew the monster didn't really feel bad. The monster was enjoying every moment.

The last thing that Justin saw was a nameplate on the zombie-soldier's coat. It said Frank. Then everything around him faded to complete blackness. Everything that was beautiful around him faded out of existence. He felt himself wake for just a moment, saw the posters in his room, saw a shadowy figure before him, and then his life faded away.

"Police!" the frantic voice of Justin's father said. "I found my boy lying in his bed this morning dead. He's dead. Someone came in last night and killed him in his sleep. All I heard was a whimper that sounded like 'Help.' I couldn't really tell, but when I went in he was dead. His face was blue, and his neck had a line bruise around it. Please help me. Please." He paused for a moment to take a drink before he gave them his address.

At the funeral Justin's family stood around and mourned the loss of such a nice—if not a little special—young boy. They said how nice he always was and how cute he always was and how he'd always made them laugh.

At the end of the procession everyone left but Justin's uncle and his father. They were the closest to the boy. They stood in silence for a few minutes until Justin's uncle put an arm around Justin's father and said, "I'm sorry that he had to die so brutally, Frank."

The thinning hair fell down onto Frank's forehead as he looked up into his brother's face and smiled, his deep blue eyes shining.

"Thanks. That means a lot."

Final Punch

The four boys sat on the side of the river, quickly downing their Jack Daniel's and Coke. They came to this spot often because it was the only place they'd found where they could be free to drink and smoke as they pleased.

"Hey, Tick, send over some more Jack, man," Colin said. "We ain't got all night, man, come on." Colin often made fun of Sam, calling him Tick and demeaning him. Colin's favorite pastime was giving Tick noogies.

"All right, it's coming over. Hold on, I'm buzzing a little here. I don't want to drop it." Sam was the loser of their clique. He often took orders and requests from the other three, trying to stay in their good graces.

Both Colin and Tom were typical jocks. They spent their time talking about pussy—how to get it and where—and Sam always sat by, intently listening. Matt was the only one of them who had carnally known a woman; but Sam was the only one who admitted to not losing his virginity, and he loved to hear Colin and Tom talk about it, his eyes brimming with adulation.

Sam slowly made his way to Colin, trying to keep his balance but not succeeding very well. He saw the rock sticking out of the ground, but it failed to register in his alcohol-addled brain. Sam took a staggering step into the rock, and all his weight shifted forward over his wavering legs, causing him to fall forward toward Colin.

None of them saw Matt reach out and grab him. They rarely saw Matt do anything under the bridge. He always seemed too contemplative to approach. He rarely said anything, mostly sticking to his drinks, downing one after another, and looking off into the distance. He almost always drank more than the others, but he never seemed to show any effects of the alcohol. This night was no exception; he quickly sat up and reached out, snagging Sam in midair.

"You better watch yourself, my man. Them snipers're gonna kill ya," Matt said, trying to sound like John Wayne and immediately and completely exiting his introspection.

"Thanks, Matt. I was just trying to get the J.D. over to Colin," Sam said, looking up with a guilty smile at all six feet and two inches of Matt's towering stature.

"I know, pilgrim. You best run 'long."

As soon as Sam tore his gaze away from Matt, Matt grabbed the Jack Daniel's bottle from his hands, quickly spun the cap off and took a deep swig, wiping his mouth with his sleeve afterward.

"Any a ya care to take me on?" Matt tossed the bottle

over to Colin, who fumbled it and screamed as the bottle shattered on the hard pan under his feet.

"Relax, the bottle was empty," Matt said, smiling at Colin, who was still looking wild-eyed at the ground where the bottle had broken.

"You drank the rest of it? There was still a quarter bottle left!" The boys, as with most boys, were prone to hyperbole.

"Relax, Colin," Matt said. "Your dad'll give us more later. Now, who's on for a little one-on-one?" He held up his fists for emphasis.

Matt loved to box. After school he would get any match he could. There was a rumor going around school that he had fought a prison guard ... and won. Behind his back the others nicknamed him Psycho.

Tom was the only one of them who would ever fight Matt. It wasn't that he was the only one who was big enough; it was that the other two were too scared. Colin had fought Matt once and, after some big talk, was knocked flat on the first punch. Sam had tried to fight Matt once, but after Matt punched him in the stomach, Sam had run away screaming. That was where Colin had gotten the nickname from; he said Sam had looked like a tick running away from a flame. That, and he was small and annoying.

"Sure, I'll take you. You've drunk enough I ought to be able to take you down," Tom said, shrugging.

"It's on. Hey, Sam, you wanna get the gloves?" Matt was the only one who called him Sam. The rest of them called him Tick.

"Yeah, hold on, I'll get 'em."

"You ready to go down, big man?" Matt said cockily, adopting his boxer's stance and dancing around Tom.

"Oh, the little man scared he gonna get hurt. He's gotta pump up his ego," Tom spouted, flexing his arms and taunting Matt.

Sam came running back with the boxing gloves in his hands, trying to keep his balance but failing once again and crashing down to the ground.

"Hey, Tick, he told you to watch out for the snipers." Colin laughed.

Matt, ignoring Colin's banter, picked up the gloves and put one on. "Minute rounds? That too long for you?" Matt gave Tom a sly smile.

"Anything you can handle, beanpole. Bring it on." Tom reached down and took up his gloves.

"So what do you want to do after Matt beats you Tom? Run off to be consoled by Palm-ela *Hand*-erson?" Colin made a masturbation motion as he spoke.

"Best sex I ever had," Tom said, getting the second glove on.

"All right, you gonna time us, Sam?" Matt asked, punching his gloves together.

"Sure. How long you guys gonna go for?"

Tom stopped dead in his tracks and looked over at Sam.

"Dumbass, didn't you just hear him say minute a round?"

"Well, yeah, but I wasn't sure if that's what you guys were going for or—"

"Minute is good, Sam. Just time us." Matt said.

"Ding-ding!" Tom said, putting his fists up.

The fight was short. Matt kept his right arm back, slowly cocking it as he jabbed Tom with his left. Tom kept his arms up, determined to win the fight, and only jabbed when he got the chance. Then Matt made his move. He dropped his left hand to his side, as if tired, and Tom, seeing his opening, swung his right fist wildly, trying to gain momentum in a roundhouse aimed at Matt's head. He never got there. Matt's cocked right hand descended and smashed Tom right above his nose, knocking him backward into the slow-moving creek.

When Matt finally pulled Tom out of the river, Colin was still laughing, and Sam was still gaping in awe.

"Jesus, man. That was strong. Fuck." Tom shook his head briefly. "Fuck!"

"You always fall for my tricks. I figure one of these days you'll figure it out," Matt said, smiling down at Tom.

"So you gonna go whack off, then?" Colin wheezed, struggling for breath through his laughter.

Tom didn't respond, just took off a dripping glove and flipped him off.

"Hey, you guys want to go do something?" Sam said abruptly, surprising them all. He'd dropped his gaze and was looking at his shoes, perturbed. "I know this place." He slowly looked up with a worried look on his face.

They pulled up to the building at about a quarter after two in the morning. It was an old mission hospital, previously used as a mental ward for the state. The building was now condemned and awaiting demolition. Tom drove up in his truck and parked three blocks away.

"So this is it, Tick?" Tom asked, looking back at the crumpled figure shoved behind the seats. Sam cocked his head so he could see around the seats and above the dashboard. He slowly nodded his head.

"Yeah, that's it. Hey, listen, maybe this is a bad idea. I mean what if the thing falls down when we're in there?"

"Don't be such a pussy, Tick," Colin said, shaking his head.

Tom opened the door and stepped out of the truck, turning just in time to see Matt jump out of the bed.

"You cats ready to go?" Tom asked with a smile, his eyes floating from the alcohol.

Matt and Colin answered by walking toward the building; Sam was still trying to climb out of the back.

"Hey, guys, wait up! Hold on—don't leave me back here, come on."

Matt turned around and grabbed Sam's arms, pulling him out of the truck and throwing him over his right shoulder. "You ready to go? This ain't gonna be a walk in the park." He said it with jest in his voice, as if he wasn't really expecting trouble.

"I guess, I just ..." Sam's voice drifted off before he finished his thought.

"Hey, if you wanna stay back and take watch duty, that's fine, Sam."

"No, I have to go in. We better get going; they're going to get there before us," Sam said motioning to Tom and Colin.

Matt put Sam down and watched him run to the other two, shaking his head as he sauntered after the three.

As Matt approached he could see fear in the others' eyes. He knew he'd have to walk them in or they would never actually go. They would talk about how they thought the place was lame and how they didn't really need to go in there, that the place was deserted anyway. Matt knew the truth: it was a terrifying edifice. It didn't matter that no one thought of the place as haunted, when he stood there and saw it in person at almost three in the morning, he knew the truth.

The building was menacing.

He knew what the others were feeling, because he felt a little of that fear himself—though he was loath to mention it. He knew the other three looked up to him. He knew they would follow him; and despite the fact that he really didn't care about going in, he knew it would be a story that would impress on Monday during free period.

"Well, then, did we come here to wait outside?" Matt asked the building, letting the question hang in the air. They all turned and looked at him, wide-eyed. This was one of the biggest reasons they loved Matt; he took them beyond their limits. He brought excitement into their lives.

He was taking them in.

Matt walked forward, grabbed the handle on the door, and quickly pulled it open.

"Shall we?" Matt said, walking in, never looking back.

"So why did you bring us here, Tick?" Colin asked, as he looked straight ahead and slowly walked into the entryway. "I mean was there a specific reason you wanted to come here, or is this just some place you jack off?" It was supposed to be funny, but Colin's voice shook with fear.

"I just thought it might be cool to come in here, you know, hang out? It might be cool. Might be better than under the bridge, smelling the crap float by us."

"Say it, man," Tom said, looking ahead the same way Colin was, trying to add some humor to *his* inflection but failing also. "Shit, just say it, man. Watching the *shit* float by us. Shit! It's easy, see? You need to get over your goddamned swearing fear."

Matt continued up ahead, walking down the dimly lit hallway, slowly looking back and forth between the walls, inspecting them. He knew Sam's reason for coming in was to show he wasn't afraid. He wanted to show his friends that nothing could scare him, maybe get a little respect. Matt thought it commendable; but there *was* something about this place, and he knew Sam wouldn't be able to handle it. There was just something in there, something that compelled Matt to keep moving forward, as if he were meant to go deeper inside.

The other three followed, leaving the door open as they entered, relishing the extra light from the streetlamps outside. They saw Matt turn the corner ahead of them. They heard the empty echo of his footsteps, then … nothing more. But then, just when the boys were wondering what Matt was up to, a bloodcurdling scream pierced the air. Tom gave Colin a worried look and then looked back at Sam.

"You think he was serious?" Tom could barely get the words out of his throat; his voice came out as a squeak.

The answer came from down the hall. Matt screamed again, but this time angrily. Tom broke into a run, tearing down the hall, dreading the corner just yards in front of him, knowing he was going to see something that he didn't want to. He knew Matt was in trouble.

He looked back right before the corner and saw Colin and Sam waiting back at the door. He couldn't believe they would just stand back there and wait to see what had happened to their friend. Tom gave a wave, indicating they should follow him, and then plunged around the corner.

At first he didn't see anything, only darkness, but soon he could tell, even in the dim light, that there were dark stains on the walls. Ahead of him was another hallway with numerous doors on either side spanning what seemed like hundreds of yards, to a window. The only illumination seemed to come from the blue moonlight flooding in that window.

"Matt? Hey man, you down here?" The statement floated out before him in the murky blue light, with only silence as an answer.

"Tom, you see him?" Colin called from behind him.

"You want to come down here and check, fag?" Tom spat back under his breath as he tried to stem his anger toward the loneliness of that dark hallway.

Tom took a few more steps into the hallway, trying to focus his eyes in the dim light. He squinted and felt a shudder run through his body. The dark splotches on the walls, he understood what they were. Blood. They were everywhere. *That can't be from the hospital,* Tom thought, but he didn't want to imagine what that thought really meant.

A door was open halfway down the hall.

"Matt! Matt, you down there?" He understood the absurdity of the statement, but he couldn't give up the hope that Matt would jump out and end the joke. He got no answer.

Tom moved to the open door and leaned up against the wall, craning his neck to see into the room and straining to bring the room into focus. Then he heard shuffling from the other side of the hallway. He snapped his head around and saw a small figure walking slowly toward him. In the shadows he couldn't make out any features, but then it raised a hand and beckoned for him to approach. Tom shut his eyes and leaned up against the doorjamb, terror freezing him in place. As he stood there, willing the figure away, a hand wrapped around his mouth, and another wrapped around his stomach. Before he could fight against it, he was dragged into the room.

Sam slowly moved into the corridor. He thought the figure down the hallway was Tom, but he couldn't really tell because the light was just too dim. He tried to wave to him, hoping that Tom would recognize that it was Sam coming to help—that it was *Sam* and not Colin. Colin had turned around and run while they were still standing outside. Without a word, he had just turned and run in the other direction. Sam knew the only thing that he could do was go into the hallway and see what was wrong. He couldn't just stand outside and wait to see, could he?

His bladder pressed against him as he walked further into the hallway, freezing him in place. He took a deep breath and tried to forget his fear. Colin was the one who had run. Colin was the one who had been scared. Besides they were probably just trying to scare him. Somehow they had come up with a plan on the way there and were tricking him. The figure in the hall quickly turned and disappeared into the room, and Sam's bladder released.

Matt lay on the ground next to the girl. The knife wound in his side burned ferociously. He could see the little girl was still alive, and that was a good sign; but he didn't know what to do. He had screamed as soon as he saw the man on top of the girl. The man had gotten up and zipped up his pants as he did so. Matt screamed the second time. He had never known himself to be so angry with anyone—especially because he didn't know exactly what was going on. He had just seen the girl lying still and the man grunting and moving. Only one thought came to mind. Matt raged and charged the man. He knew it was a mistake; he couldn't even see his adversary very well, and he knew to never let his anger take control—but it had. He had charged at the man, throwing a punch, not seeing the knife in his hand. The blade flashed a dull blue light, and in an instant it was hilt-deep in Matt's side. Instantly he fell. He heard the man cough slightly and suck saliva back into his mouth. Matt looked at the girl, trying to gather his thoughts, knowing that his friends were in trouble, knowing that this girl was hurt. This small, innocent girl.

Tom was twirled around by the strong hands and felt something very hot thrust into his stomach, making his legs go weak. He looked up into the man's face and saw dark eyes, an unshaven face, and rotten teeth. His breath smelled like a sewer.

"You here to join yo' frien, ma' facka?" the man hissed into Tom's face with a heavy drawl.

Tom could do nothing but groan. His legs started to give out, and his stomach blossomed in pain. He felt the blade inside of him, wiggling around, sending searing pain every time it moved.

Tom looked away from the man and saw Matt lying on the floor next to a girl. His legs finally gave out. He felt himself falling to the floor. He felt the knife slide out of his body, slowly expanding the wound with its serrated edge. Tom's knees hit the floor.

The man cackled from above him and then turned back to the girl lying on the ground.

Tom let out a wheeze and raised his arm, unsure of his own intentions, just hoping help would come from somewhere. The man noticed Tom raising his arm, and without turning, he mule-kicked him in the face. Tom fell backward, watching the room spin and wondering why he had agreed to come along.

Matt watched as the man pulled Tom into the room, and fresh anger flushed back into his veins, making his blood flow faster and making his wound ooze with renewed vigor. But despite the free flow of blood, he felt his mind clear. He watched the man stab Tom and then turn and kick him. The man turned to look at Matt and then he unzipped his fly and took his pants back down, looking straight at Matt while he slowly masturbated and got down on his knees in front of the girl.

Matt fought back the anger and waited for the man to stop looking at him.

"Tom? Matt? Are you guys down here?" Sam asked in a meek voice from down the hall.

The man turned around and bared his teeth like a feral animal, letting out a grunt of disgust at the voice.

Matt took his opportunity. He quickly rolled to his back, and kicked both legs out, trying to make contact with the man's testicles.

Matt extended his legs with as much force as he could muster, ignoring the flaring pain that blossomed in his side. Unfortunately the man moved at exactly the right moment. Instead of connecting with the man's disfigured testicles, Matt hit his right thigh, sending the man off balance and causing him to fall backward onto Tom.

Matt staggered to his feet as quickly as he could, trying to beat the man to his feet, but when Matt finally got upright the man was already up, ready, with knife in hand.

"We gots a fighta, huh?" the man hissed.

"Bring it on, fucker."

Matt got set up in his boxing stance, with his left arm forward, throwing a few exploratory jabs at the man. With every jab, the man attempted to slash Matt's wrist. Sam entered the doorway and squealed when he saw what was happening in the room: a stranger with no pants on, holding a knife, fighting with Matt.

Matt kept jabbing at the man, taking the slashes to his arm, ignoring the flashing pain, but with each jab, his raised right fist cocked back even further.

"You likin' this, pretty?" the man said, smiling and showing his rotten teeth.

Sam stood in the doorway, amazed at the sight, when he felt something pull on his pissed-soaked pants. Sam looked down at Tom; blood was running from his nose, and he had a glazed look in his eyes.

"Get help," Tom whispered before he fell back down to the floor.

Matt jabbed the man one last time, comfortable with the power he'd generated with his right arm, and then dropped his left arm, letting the man into his open chest. The man lunged with the knife at the same time Matt unleashed his sledgehammer of a right arm. They made contact at the same time, the knife gently sliding into Matt's chest, while Matt crushed the man's nose, spraying a fine mist of blood in a halo around the man's head. The man fell backward in conjunction with Matt.

Sam watched the two fighters fall and then ran off, terrified of the knife sticking out of Matt's chest and the glazed look in his eyes.

Matt lurched on the ground, listening to the rapist's growls of anger. Pain flared in his lungs, and when he looked down he saw the cause. The six-inch Gerber blade was still sticking out of his chest. Matt slowly reached for the knife, while turning his head toward Tom.

Tom reacted to the man falling by trying to roll on top of him, laying the rapist out with punches. Matt watched with pride as Tom valiantly pinned the man down and raised his fists in fury.

"You're gonna die, fucker!"

Matt could see the fire blazing in Tom's eyes, but he realized a moment later they weren't going to make it. The rapist, somehow, already had another knife in his hand.

Tom swung his right fist down, and the knife came up to meet his neck. Surprise appeared in Tom's eyes, and his limbs went limp. The rapist threw him off, ripping the knife out in the process. A fountain of blood poured from Tom's neck.

"Na, pretty, time fur you. Not niiice to en-tee-rupt whilst one's fuckin.'"

The rapist began to rub his penis, his hands wet with blood. Then he got down on his knees and crawled toward Matt, the knife clutched in his free hand.

Matt said nothing, waiting for his opportunity. He knew he would only get one. He closed his eyes and waited.

One

Two

Three

A hand on his foot. Knife slowly scraping the skin.

Four

Up to thigh. Matt twitched his arm.

Five

The hand grabbed his belt, and Matt erupted into a flurry. He whipped his hand to his chest and ripped the knife out, screaming and coughing blood while doing so. The rapist smiled, relishing Matt's pain, until Matt kicked hard and upward into the rapist's genitals.

"Fuckin' aghhh! Fuck!" He grabbed his testicles and fell to his side, while Matt swung the knife up hard, straight to his temple. A wet, scraping sound echoed in the room. To Matt it sounded like a butcher preparing a steak, and immediately he felt sick.

The only sound the man made was a clicking in his

throat. Then he fell, the death rattle continuing as he hit the ground.

Matt looked at the fading light in Tom's eyes and smiled, intently listening for the wail of sirens.

Tom smiled back, and in the hazy malaise of his memory he thought of all the times he had spent with Matt and Sam and Colin. All the times they had joked about sex and girls and fighting. All the boasts and lies about their prowess. None of it was wasted. It was all meant for here and now. They had done something grand together, the four of them. The ones who got into trouble for being drunk at school. The ones who sneaked liquor and pills from their parents. They had stopped this man. They were heroes.

In his last moment, Tom felt pride in being Matt's friend and pride in his actions. Pride in wandering through the teenage wasteland and coming out a man on the other side.

All-Night Diner

Part I
Raven's Diner

The diner lay in a desolate wilderness ten miles from the town of Cheyenne, Wyoming. It was a way station for weary travelers as they made their way through the depressing flats of the Great Plains. Its original name was Capote's, which was displayed on a carved wooden sign hanging above the door. Its owner was Jacques Capote, who had built the place as a front for a drug- and arms-trading post. He dealt with gangs and delinquents and bribed the police, all the while developing a taste for cooking and turning Capote's into a place coveted by the passing trucking and biking crowd, who could pick up, not only a decent bite to eat, but some uppers for the road. It wasn't until Jacques's beautiful wife and newborn son were killed in an altercation with police in the diner that he decided to change his career and, in the interest of safety, the bar's name.

The story goes that the funeral for his family was delayed because a raven landed on his son's casket. He spent hours staring at the raven, screaming at anyone who tried to move the bird. He raved that it was the spirit of his dead son. Later that night after the bird flew away and the woman and the boy were buried, the raven returned to Jacques. It sat on his windowsill and, if you believe some who tell the tale, spoke to Jacques. It gave him instructions.

The next day the carved wooden sign, which travelers strained to find, came down. The day after that, a new neon sign, which read "Raven's Diner," went up. The day after the new diner opened, ownership of the bar went to Jorge Calaveras, a man who frequented the diner. On the fourth day Jacques put a shotgun in his mouth and displayed his brains on the window of his newly christened Raven's Diner.

Some said the place was cursed. Some said it was haunted. Some said it had the best corned beef hash in the Great Plains. No matter which story you believe, it was in this place that seven people met and spent the night in a diner with a view of the edge of the world.

Part II
The Lovers

"*Fuck you!* I'm not going to jail! I didn't do anything wrong!" the greasy biker said from the other side of the diner. Robert looked at the man from out of the corner of his eye, just to make sure he wasn't going to ruin the night, and then turned and looked back at Tanya.

Robert drank his coffee in abstinent silence, fingering the ring he had brought to the tryst. He looked across the stained Formica into Tanya's brown eyes. There were slight crow's-feet at the corners of her eyes, which had once caught excess makeup and made caked lines, spindles that crept away from the corners of her eyes. She had used the makeup to hide the bruises her dead boyfriend had given her.

But Robert had saved her from all that. She no longer wore makeup; in fact whenever she passed a counter with a young woman attempting to sell it, she would shy away and hide in Robert's arms. That night was their anniversary. It was a year free from makeup and abuse.

That was the reason Robert had brought her back to Raven's. He wanted her to stand in the diner she used to frequent with her abusive boyfriend and face her fears. Once she did he was going to have the waitress serve her favorite dish and then present the giant diamond that weighed down his pocket. She amazed him with her vitality and stubbornness. He wondered sometimes why she had stayed for so long with a man who abused her.

Robert surmised that if he were to raise a hand to her she would tear his head off, but then again, he thought, maybe being beaten for a solid year is what it took for some people to finally stand up for themselves.

He remembered the first time he had seen those eyes.

A year earlier he was on a poorly run PR tour for his new book *The Ingredients of Life*, which featured a poor writer traveling from city to city and trying to find his purpose. The protagonist had sex with prostitutes, did drugs in Portland flophouses, tipped cows while tripping on acid in the Wyoming plains, had a drinking contest with a senator from Texas, and eventually died of a gunshot wound in a cemetery in El Paso.

Cheyenne was as far as his publicity company was willing to pay for him to go, and Robert wasn't sure if that was a reflection of their budget or their opinion of his writing.

He had been passing the quaint little Raven's when his Dodge Dart's radiator boiled over. Six months later he would tell Tanya that their meeting had been serendipitous. If his writing were any better, they never would have met.

Her makeup application was thicker that day than it normally was. Her boyfriend, whom she called by his nickname, Chopper, had beaten her especially badly the night before. He would usually focus his efforts on her stomach because it brought fewer questions from people; it was not that he really worried about such things, but he found it easier to avoid questions altogether.

Robert had looked at her, taken note of the obvious swamp-colored distortion of her skin tone, and sighed in absent empathy. She saw him looking and gave him a slight and self-conscious smile and then raised one of her hands to cover as much of her face as she could.

Robert had written a novel called *Life: Intransigent* three years earlier in which the main character was a battered woman. He felt it would be untruthful or perhaps somewhat unrealistic to write about the experience the woman had in the moment, so he focused on the battering as a memory, something as fleeting as a dream, used only as backstory to give a greater understanding of the woman's decision to avoid male contact. She was a villain because of it. A cold, calculating bank robber who couldn't understand affection because it was something she had never had or at least couldn't remember having. The book was a perfect statement of Robert's ignorance of the broad range of human emotion.

So when he saw her eating dinner with the large man in the leather vest, when he saw her look at him and smile, he smiled back and then focused on his meatloaf.

Throughout his meal he noticed her stealing glimpses at him. Every so often he would look at her directly, and she would smile and very coyly look at the ground.

Robert's assumption was that she recognized him from one of his book's dust jackets, but that was only partially true. She did recognize him; she'd read all of his books, and while she thought his writing was a little subpar at times, she also thought he understood what it meant to be in peril. Every story he wrote had characters in extraordinary circumstances. In *The Particles of Faith* a priest is excommunicated from his church for alcoholism and travels the country as a preacher, stealing and healing along the way. In *Dodger* a young man is imprisoned for killing a man when he's eighteen and spends his time in jail plotting escape. The list went on.

So she locked eyes on him and tried to convey her situation, covering her bruises only that first time and giving him a view of what she represented through her body language.

Robert, whose longest relationship had lasted only a year, ignored her obvious flirtations. He felt mildly uncomfortable, as if he was starring in a third-rate *Dukes of Hazzard* knock-off, in which the large biker would turn around and beat him for staring at his girl. Her gazes were just *so* resolute.

When he finished his meatloaf he got up and gave her a shy grin as he made his way to the bathroom. He didn't know it at the time, but this small, furtive glance was his downfall. She had been desperately trying to gain his attentions because her perception was that all writers had money and she thought the best way to escape the choking grasp of Chopper was to run away with a man who could solve problems through money. Money could fix anything. He didn't seem to be responding to her though, and as his meatloaf began to disappear from his plate, her hope began to drop like the first dead leaf of autumn. Slow but steady.

Then, on his way to the bathroom, he smiled at her, and she saw her shot. She excused herself from Chopper's side (he didn't even register her leaving, as he was busy wolfing down his own portion of meatloaf) and demurely made her way to the bathroom doors where she waited for him to come back out.

Robert peed languorously, searching his mind for ways to avoid contact with her. Robert was a pacifist at heart, and the thought of confrontation scared him. His big plan was to exit the bathroom, throw money down on his table and nod his head at her, so when she met him at the entrance to the bathroom, he let out a little squeak under his breath.

She stood before him with her arm on the doorjamb, her legs spread, her lips full, and her eyes held a worldly and knowing gaze. She handed him a piece of paper, and then she leaned forward and grabbed the back of his neck, pulling his lips to hers. Her lips were glossy, and she tasted of coffee.

The kiss lasted only for a moment, and when it was over she slid her hand from the back of his head to his cheek. She looked, not away, but down as she did this. She wanted to show him she understood what she was doing was wrong. She wanted to show him she felt shame for her actions, but the hand on his cheek was meant to display that, no matter how wrong it was, she *wanted* it.

There were no words in their first interaction (unless you count Robert's squeak). It ended there, with her walking back and sitting next to Chopper and him fulfilling his earlier plan. He walked over to his table, threw down his money, and then walked out of the diner. The one change in his plan came at the door (next to the neon sign) when he turned back to catch one last glimpse of her. She was looking back at him, her makeup-caked face wrinkling with expectancy.

When Robert got back to the hotel, he opened the note. There were two words and ten numbers. *Tanya Pearson 803-567-8956.*

My God, he thought, *this is like a story I would write!*
He called her back the next day.

Initially Tanya used him. Their first meeting she found out he had no money but that he seemed to be willing to do anything for her. He was like an angel sent from heaven. He was everything she wanted in a man. He was considerate, he listened, and most important, he didn't beat her.

They met secretly for months, always talking briefly about their separate lives and then spiritedly copulating when the conversation ran down.

Robert was in love from the first moment. He loved her small-town mentality and her ineffable compulsion to be needed. Her life didn't seem to have purpose, and she was slowly slipping down into depression. Chopper only seemed to need her as a focus for his outpouring of lust and aggression. Robert though, accepted her and empathized with her. He hated Chopper and often talked about giving him a piece of his mind. (Of course Tanya always took this lightly because Robert was so soft-spoken and Chopper was three times his size.) But when the evenings devolved into intercourse he quickly forgot his anger.

Three months after their first meeting Tanya came to a realization. She was pregnant. She decided to wait to tell both Chopper and Robert until she knew when conception had been. The only way she was going to keep it was if it were Robert's; if she couldn't definitively identify the father she was going to abort it. There wasn't any reason to chance having Chopper's baby.

A few months later she began to show, and immediately Chopper was proud. When he found out, he grabbed Tanya in a headlock and gave her noogies, laughing and whooping. He said it was a miracle; the doctors had told him (after a fight he got into when he was twenty in which he had been kicked in the testicles repeatedly) that he would probably never be able to conceive a baby; his testicles were just too damaged.

Robert was elated when she told him he was going to be a father. He held her tight and kissed her deeply. That night after they made love she left him to return to Chopper, and he began to formulate a plan to get his new love away from her tyrannical boyfriend.

When Tanya got home she was dismayed to find Chopper even more drunk than usual. He had gone to his local hangout Stephanie's (a bar owned by the head of the Vagabonds, his biker gang) and gotten free drinks in congratulations all night long. Chopper tried to fuck Tanya that night but because of the alcohol was unable to attain an erection. She tried to buffer his ego by sucking him, but he remained skin taffy.

Chopper, who had never dealt with embarrassment

well, beat Tanya until she was unconscious. He tried to keep his blows to her face and torso, avoiding her stomach so as to save his unborn son (he had no idea that, not only was the baby not his, it wasn't even a boy); unfortunately in his stupor he eventually forgot she was pregnant and laid a few very well-placed kicks, killing the unborn baby.

When Tanya woke she was lying in a pool of blood and immediately knew what had happened. She called Robert and told him about the beating, weeping and sobbing into the receiver. They agreed on a meeting spot to discuss what they would do. She wouldn't have cared if it were Chopper's baby, but because it was Robert's, it opened her eyes to the reality of her situation. She was not living a real life but in some kind of bizarre, warped Wonderland. She came to the realization that she was the only one who could change her circumstances. She was the one who would have to act. She just didn't realize Robert would be so willing to help.

"Let's kill the son of a bitch." He said it coldly, with a determined look in his eyes. Tanya thought she saw his nostrils flare.

They came up with the plan together. They would call a rival gang, the Sons of Chaos, and tell them Chopper was selling on their property out in the forest by Lake Meneloua. Robert called Chopper, explaining that he was a friend of one of Tanya's high school friends, and set up a date to acquire some crank.

It was the perfect plan, and it worked just how they thought it would. Tanya stayed home so she would have plausible deniability, and Robert went out to meet Chopper. Robert got to the meeting spot (out in the woods next to an old run-down boathouse) early and was surprised when Chopper got there ten minutes before the scheduled time. Chopper didn't say a word during the transaction; he just looked at Robert, staring deep into his eyes. They exchanged money for goods, and Chopper took a few steps backward, wearily eyeing Robert. Chopper made it a hundred feet when he stopped in his tracks. Robert, knowing the rival gang must have started their move, began to slowly walk in Chopper's direction.

The kill shot came quick. They didn't give him a chance to speak; they didn't even give him a chance to run. He took two .22 caliber bullets to the head and dropped to the forest floor. As Robert walked past, giving the body a wide berth, he raised a hand to the man holding the gun. The man nodded back.

Four months later Tanya and Robert sat again in Raven's diner. Tanya had gone to Chopper's funeral and then had disappeared, leaving a note behind that said she was too heartbroken to stick around. She and Robert had been living out of hotels and hostels ever since. She never dreamed her life would be lived in hotels, but she relished every minute of it. The freedom and liberation that came from the road was like nothing she had ever experienced. She felt like she had been released from prison.

Robert pulled the ring from his pocket and brought it to his lap. He smiled at Tanya, who smiled back; it was a look of complicit joy, and it made Robert's heart sing.

Robert was so wrapped up in mentally practicing his proposal that he didn't notice the short, fat, balding man walk into the diner behind him. It wasn't until Tanya's eyes widened as the man raised his arm and pointed a Glock at the back of Robert's head that Robert realized something was wrong.

Robert turned slightly, saw the man's face, and said one word before the bullet destroyed his brain and he collapsed into a pile of useless organics in his seat.

"You!" His publicist would hardly be happy to hear this was his last word.

Part III
The Privileged

Abraham Gelding Winslock watched in horror as the short, ugly, fat man barged in the front door and pulled the trigger. The sight of Robert's head exploding out across the table and covering Tanya was too much for him. Abe turned to the window with his hand daintily covering his mouth, holding in the high-pitched screech he felt building within him. It was not the first time he had seen someone's brain exit his body.

Abe was descended from old money. His father was a banker who had graduated from Harvard at the top of his class. His father before him had done the same. The Winslock money came from the early 1800s when the first Abraham founded New England Trust, which rivaled

Bank of Italy in prestige. The original Abe's son, Tristan, had sold the trust to the Bank of Italy (which shortly afterward changed its name to Bank of America) and became a millionaire. That money had been invested and saved, and it slowly grew to immense proportions.

Abe's father was the first to branch out into work outside of investing and became a philanthropist of the first order. He spent his time building soup kitchens and hostels for the unfortunate. His plan was for Abe to follow suit, after he finished Harvard of course, and continue the prestige of the Winslock name. For the entirety of his life Abe had believed in these goals, and he strove for them. As a boy he had been at the top of his class in his academy and had near-perfect test scores. He was accepted into Harvard, and for the first two years he excelled.

Abe was a quiet boy, unassuming and polite. He seemed to live to please people and to serve. His desire to please began at a very early age when he realized he was gay. His father took him to a brothel (a high-end, very expensive bordello known only to rich men and ignored by their wives) and let him pick out anyone he chose. Abe couldn't choose, so his father did for him. When the prostitute took him to her room, she instantly recognized the problem.

"Does he know, honey? Is he trying to make sure you're straight, or is he trying to make you fuck it out of yourself?" She was crude and beautiful, but the only love Abe felt for her was for the elaborate trappings of her trade.

He vowed from that moment that he wouldn't let his father know and that he'd do anything he could to please him—and that meant hiding his homosexuality. Abe saw his sexual preference as a problem, an issue he was unable to resolve, so he decided to ignore it. As a result he grew up shy and antisocial but extremely intelligent. The quality time he should have spent with friends, he instead spent languishing in the comforting embraces of Proust, Dickinson, Dickens, and the Brontë sisters.

He didn't branch out of his bubble until his second year at Harvard. He met another boy who seemed interested in him, in the way that Abe deemed only appropriate between man and woman.

Charles Van Pugh was a beautiful boy: six feet tall and the perfect Aryan. His hair was delicately cropped and framed his deep blue eyes and creamy skin.

Charles was the captain of the basketball team and loved by everyone at school. The women coveted him, and the men envied him. He spent his nights doing anything he wanted and his days sleeping. His father, Vincent Van Pugh, was a man of fairly new money. When Vincent was ten his father had started his own insurance company, growing his moderate salary to unforeseen levels. Vincent took over the family business when he turned thirty, and his plans for Charles were the same.

Charles, knowing his fate, accepted that he had a direct path and decided at a very young age that he would need to live his life as fully as possible, because once he turned that fateful age, his life as he knew it would be over. So Vincent took care of everything for him. He spent his time at the office and had his lawyers handle every issue his firebrand of a son had, eventually deciding, though, that Charles was just too much of a handful. Vincent slowly backed out of Charles's life. His only interjections were to hand Charles favors, like acceptance to Harvard despite his straight Ds, and his trust fund, which totaled 8.8 million dollars (which he would receive when he turned twenty-five).

Charles, in his all-knowing, twenty-year-old wisdom, decided that sex was the gateway to everything he wanted, and since he was lucky enough to be princely bred, things generally worked out for him. He fucked girls for rides. He fucked guys for favors. He fucked his teachers for grades and the school administrators to erase his records. It was during this promiscuous streak that Charles met Abe.

To Charles it was just a fuck for homework, but to Abe it was the first real person who seemed to take notice of him. Charles was Abe's first, and because of this he fell for him hard. Abe felt he loved Charles and forgave everything he did. He knew Charles slept with everyone he could; but Abe just liked being in his company, so he put up with it all. Abe was just waiting for the possibility that Charles would see how much he loved him and return the emotion.

Charles's bad behavior and Abe's love for him were how they came to be in the diner on that night.

One month before Robert was killed, Abe met Charles at a party. Charles told Abe that the only way he would continue to fuck him was if he was high, so Abe met him there with a baggie of weed and a six-pack of beer. Abe spent the better part of the day trying to score an eighth, and when he did, he grossly overpaid. It was just something he had never done before; and the dealer, recognizing his innocence raped his wallet.

That night Abe's plan seemed to be holding up well. Charles smoked most of the bag during the night, sharing with other people, and intermittently drinking his beers until he decided that there was nothing else of interest (in actuality the girl he was after had left with another guy) and so he wanted to go home. Abe offered to drive since he hadn't done anything but admire Charles's perfect jawline, but Charles would have nothing of it. He grabbed the keys from Abe's hand and jumped in his Aston Martin. Abe barely had time to get in before the car zipped away.

It took Charles ten miles to realize he didn't have his headlights on, and the whole time Abe sat clutching the sides of his seat. Charles snapped the lights on and then looked over at Abe and smiled. Charles could see that Abe was terrified, and he relished it.

"Relax, baby. It's all copasetic. I know what'll calm you down." His eyes wavered, and he didn't look at the road, while he unzipped his pants.

"Charles, please." Abe was scared, and his lisp came through more strongly than it normally did.

"You know you want to." Charles didn't even look Abe in the eye; he just grabbed the back of Abe's head and pulled it to his crotch.

Abe didn't say anything; he was actually a little scared by the strength that Charles put behind it, slamming Abe's face down into his flaccid penis. Later he would chastise himself for not putting up a fight; but at that time (actually every time Charles was horny) Abe felt needed and wanted by someone he was attracted to, and he couldn't stop. But the more time that he spent blowing Charles the more flaccid his penis seemed to become.

It confused Abe because Charles kept speaking as if he liked it. "Yeah, bitch! You suck that cock!" There were even a few groans thrown in there, so Abe just kept at it. Abe didn't realize, though, that in Charles's state he *still* wasn't watching the road, and less than a minute into the act, the car jolted in conjunction with a loud bang, as if someone had punched the hood of the car.

Abe whipped his head up, and Charles slammed his foot on the brakes.

"Holy shit." Charles's voice was very soft and very calm.

"Whatthefuckwasthat?" Abe said, staring at Charles, too scared to look out the window.

Charles didn't say anything. He just gripped the steering wheel and looked through the windshield.

Abe retched when he dared look through the windshield. There was red goo all over the glass, almost like pumpkin innards died red with little bits of gray sludge and white fragments dispersed throughout.

"That little girl, man. She just popped!" Charles

looked out through the windshield, and Abe vomited again when he heard the windshield wipers start.

Charles only waited until the windshield was clear, and then he took the car out of park and began to drive away. Abe never said anything. He was terrified, and his stomach was threatening to continue its regurgitation; so he kept his face between his legs.

Charles took Abe to his dormitory and dropped him at the entrance. He didn't wait for Abe to say anything; he drove away while the door was still open. Abe got one last glance of Charles's flaccid penis as the stained Aston Martin drove away.

That night he didn't sleep. He waited for the police to come to his door and arrest him. He waited for Charles to come and kill him, for fear that Abe would squeal. He waited, but he didn't do anything. He didn't call the police. He didn't call his parents. He didn't know what to do, and he saw that girl's brains sprayed across the windshield every time he closed his eyes.

He stayed in his dorm room for a week, waiting. His roommate stopped coming home. His clothes stank, he didn't shower, and he was a wreck. He felt dirty inside his mind. He felt constantly sick and restless, exhausted and sleepless, bored and terrified. He didn't know what to do.

Then after a week he ventured out to take a shower late at night. There was no one in the hallway, and no one in the shower. It was quieter than he'd ever experienced. He crept down the hallway, making sure to be quiet, and jumped under the warm water. He felt relief wash over him. He went over the events of the night and decided he shouldn't get into trouble. After all he never even saw the girl. It could have been a deer. Charles was so trashed that night it could have been anything. He gave himself countless excuses for what it was and took all responsibility off his shoulders. When he got back to his room, he fell fast asleep.

He went on with his normal life after that.

He didn't give that little girl another thought for a week.

But then one night the fog started to roll in over Harvard Yard. He could see the fog moving in closer, thickening and congealing the air. He peered out into the morass and saw a lone figure standing next to a tree, leaning on the tree to hold its weight.

The fog and his tortured mind blurred the reality of the situation, and when the figure began to walk through the milky cloud, Abe thought for sure it was the girl. His rational mind left him, and fear of being tormented by the girl's ghost seeped into his conscious mind. He imagined her half-shattered body shuffling toward him, scraping a useless leg behind her as she slowly made her way to his window.

Abe shut his eyes and sank down to the floor underneath the window. He could almost feel the fog beating against the dorm.

He was about to stand again to take another peek when he heard harsh breathing coming from the other side of the window.

He flatted himself against the floor and looked up to the window. He could see hands cupped over eyes ... blue eyes. Charles's eyes.

Abe lept up and threw open the window, startling Charles. Abe reached out through the window and slapped Charles, and then brought his face close and gave him a soft kiss on the lips. Abe's emotions were running wild, and he didn't know what to think or how to act when he finally looked Charles in the eyes.

Through the whole ordeal Charles never said a word, and it wasn't until Abe was finished scolding him that he realized Charles was as white as a sheet.

The story came out in a slow, measured cadence. Charles was at basketball practice when a man in a suit showed up and gave a letter to his coach. After practice the coach handed the note to Charles and gave him a sympathetic pat on the back. Charles ignored it and went to the locker room. Once there, amidst his fellow teammates he opened the envelope, which had a Polaroid in it. It was a very clear picture, taken at night with the flash to maximize the carnage. It was the girl, her head half gone, the chest caved in, and one leg a twisted branch with bone gleaming in the light of the camera flash. On the back of the picture a sentence was written out: "Raven's Diner at 7:00 PM Tuesday."

Abe was thinking about that night as Robert's brains splayed across Tanya. He recalled the thick fog rolling in from the darkness. They had taken a step out of reality, a ride given by the fog. Now they were stuck in the diner with a man who had already killed some one else ... and they had been *told* to come here. Someone knew what they had done and had set them up.

Oh, God, thought Abe. *What if it's the man with the gun?*

Part IV
The Prostitute

The businessman who'd followed her here looked at her first when the gun went off. She saw that much right away. The two slightly homoerotic college studs never even gave her a second glance. The smaller, effeminate one (Mary thought of him as the receiver) jumped up in his seat and screamed like an arachnophobia-prone prepubescent girl while the larger, muscular one (this one was the giver) just sneered in disgust.

The businessman was the first to react. He leapt from his seat and tackled the tubby gunman, spilling them both onto the floor. She could see them both struggling for the gun, but the businessman seemed much better in such physical disputes. The woman who was with the dead guy was screaming, and the pitch hurt Mary's ears. That bitch had to calm down.

Mary slid to the back of the seat in her corner of the diner and thought back on her night. *One of the most fucked-up nights I've ever had.* She had to get out of this diner before someone else died and more important before the police got here. A crime scene was no place for a twice-convicted prostitute.

She looked out into the dark, black night and noticed the deep green sign for Interstate 82 down at the end of the driveway to the diner. She looked longingly at the road and thanked God that she had been as lucky in her life as she had been; all she needed now was an extension of that luck so she could get out of there.

Of course her luck hadn't always been there; when she was a little girl she had been decidedly unlucky.

She grew up without a father, and her mother had always told her he had died when she was very young. He had been a firefighter and had died in a burning blaze when Mary was still in her womb. He was a policeman who had saved a group of nuns during a bank robbery while Mary was being born. He was a priest who died while exorcising a demon from a young girl. The story changed weekly.

Mary's mother faked at being religious. She often told Mary she was named after the mother of God, because she was meant for great things. She was meant for much better things than living at the trailer park with her mother.

Mary and her mother were very poor and to supplement the meager money Mary's mother, Petunia, made at the Laundromat, she dated and tried to find men who would be willing to support her. It was something she was very bad at.

Mary was shown early that physical and verbal abuse were just part of what happened in relationships. To her it was the normal course of life. Petunia's first boyfriend used to come home from his construction job and slap her if dinner wasn't on the table. He used to put tape on Mary's mouth if she cried. Then one day he hit Petunia too hard, and she fell, cutting her face on a plate she was drying. Mary's mother told her she needed to be beautiful always because the man who had been so kind as to provide them with food had left because she got a scar from the plate and he didn't like to look at it.

Mary also learned, very young, that a woman has her place, and she learned it over again in a brand-new way when she turned eleven. Her mother's boyfriend at the time was a slightly overweight, greasy, stay-at-home father figure. He'd gotten a million dollars off a frivolous lawsuit and used the money to be a disgusting slob and waste his time on a couch. Mary had just gotten into third grade. Her mother was taking less and less interest in her, being too overwhelmed by the pressures of life and having a child, so she began to drink. Heavily. Most nights her mother drank with her slob of a boyfriend (who slept all day, that is, when he wasn't watching TV), and they tried, loudly, to fuck. Most nights he was too drunk to get it up, but one night after her mother had passed out in a drunken stupor, this drunken slob of a boyfriend entered Mary's room and told her what good daughters did for their fathers, told her what men look for in a woman ... and he never had trouble maintaining an erection with *her*.

Things continued on like this for years until the slob left them. With the money gone and work the only apparent option, Mary's mother made a hard decision. She sent letters out and tried to find Mary's *actual* father. While doing this, she sent Mary out to the street to get money. Petunia knew what Mary did with the slob and thought of Mary as a real woman by then. She had a brief thought that *maybe* she had named her daughter after that other biblical Mary and then started to drink and forgot the whole thing.

That was how Mary spent her early life, going from one john to another, making a pittance and spending it on pleather outfits.

Petunia died when Mary was seventeen. She literally drank herself to death. It took Mary three days to realize that Petunia was dead, and when she finally understood, she closed her mother's eyes, slapped her face, and left the trailer, never to return.

The night she ended up at the diner started off the same as any of her other nights. She was at home getting dressed when she got a call from a new john. She often kept her regulars on speed dial just in case she needed some extra money; also it better prepared her for their special requests.

The call she got was cryptic and intriguing. It asked her to meet at an address, and if the john was pleased, payment would be copious. Mary didn't know what that meant, but it sounded promising.

She arrived at a nice-looking townhouse and honked twice in quick succession as instructed. Two minutes later a man in a pressed, double-pleated suit exited the house and made great care to lock all three deadbolts on the door before securing the standard knob lock. Mary took no notice because she was busy practicing her pouty look in the rearview mirror.

When the man got in the passenger seat he didn't say anything but laid his hands meekly in his lap and lowered his head slightly, looking down at his carefully manicured hands. Mary looked over at him and smiled at his innocence.

"Where to, baby?"

He looked up at her and purposefully blinked twice.

"Go directly to Interstate 82 and exit on Meneloua Pass and park by the boathouse. Do not speed."

He blinked one more time and then looked back down at his hands.

"Honey, the only speeding I'm gonna cause is when your blood rushes to your dick." She licked her lips in a lubricious and vaguely vulgar way and put the car into gear.

He didn't say a thing during the entire drive down to the lake. He just kept his hands in his lap and kept his eyes trained them.

When she put the car into park she turned the volume up slightly on the radio and turned to him.

"What can I do for you, baby?" Her ignorance was due to her luck. She had been doing this for years now, and she had never had an issue with anyone. She never had a pimp, but then again she never really needed one. No one ever gave her any trouble, and when they did they never came back to her again.

He didn't raise his head. "I want you to take off your top. I want you to rip it off." He spoke fast and out of breath as if he were turned on already.

Mary smiled and slowly lifted her shirt. "Is this what you like, baby?"

"*I said rip it off!*" Spittle flew from his lips, and he raised his eyes from his hands. They burned with fire, and drool was falling from his lips. She felt her luck drain. She leaned back against the window and let her satin blouse fall back into place. "*Why do they always* make *me do it?*" the man said.

Mary didn't know if he was talking to himself or to her, but she didn't want to stick around to find out. She reached behind her and tried for the handle of the door.

"*You don't leave!*" This time she knew he was talking to her, and she felt his strangely large hand cup the crown of her head. "Why do they always try to leave when I'm teaching them a lesson?" He whispered in her ear just before he smashed her face against the window.

For the first time in her life she realized that the abuse she had previously thought normal in a relationship was far darker and more menacing. She wondered if her mother feared, as she did now, that the man abusing her might be trying to kill her. Her heart sang for her poor dead mother as she slipped from consciousness.

When Mary came to she was lying on the side of the road. She had her purse with her, and her attire seemed in order, nothing ripped or cut. She looked about, trying to get her bearings, and noticed she was no longer at Lake Meneloua. She was sitting on the side of Interstate 82. Groggily, she stood and started to walk down the highway, unaware in the darkness of where exactly she was along the interstate.

She walked for nearly two miles before a car passed, and she was grateful when it did. While traveling she had the distinct feeling of being watched, and at one point, she thought she could hear the crack of a twig from out in the woods. She ignored it, though, and walked all the faster.

The old Ford Taurus stopped just a few yards ahead of her, and she ran to the car, not in elation for the possibility of getting a ride, but in fear of the man who had hurt her, who was probably following her in the woods.

She whipped open the door, plopped into the passenger side, and shut the door. "Thanks, mister."

"Holy shit! What happened?" The man had long hair and looked a little greasy, but she felt safer with him than without him.

She looked quickly into the rearview mirror and was not surprised when she saw her face was covered in bruises, but what disturbed her even more was the bandage on her forehead. She reached up and lightly touched it, wincing at the lacing pain.

"Please drive. I'll tell you on the way." She glanced

into the woods to see if she could see the man and then breathed a sigh of relief as the car started moving.

They pulled into the parking lot at Raven's fifty miles later after the man, who introduced himself as Tommy, told her she looked as if she needed some food in her, just like he did.

They were there for a short time, not quite long enough to get food, when the businessman walked in. Mary's new john immediately started to seem nervous.

"That fucking guy has been staring at us since we walked in here. Is he a cop?"

Mary turned around and looked the businessman in the eye.

"He looks like a horny old fogey—that's what he looks like." He didn't, though. In fact, Mary found him very attractive, and when she looked at him, he stared straight back into her eyes and smiled slightly. She felt her heart flutter and the strange need to have the businessman hold her.

"He better not be a cop. Are you setting me up? You can't get anything on me. I'm just an innocent bystander!" His voice started to break, and Mary realized for the first time she had never propositioned him. All men were the same. Even if they did something nice for you they wanted something out of it. Maybe he thought he could get it for free if he took her out to dinner.

"This isn't *Pretty Woman*, pal. You're still gonna have to pay." She turned back to find him half-standing.

"*Fuck you*! I'm not going to jail! I didn't do anything

wrong!" He was loud but not terribly so. She hoped the people on the other side of the restaurant couldn't hear him. She felt strangely ashamed that the businessman could.

She didn't make a move to stop him, and he charged out the front door, sneering at the businessman as he went by. The businessman never took his eyes off her. He ignored Tommy completely.

Mary looked at him and had a distinct feeling of déjà vu. Something about him seemed familiar. It could have been one of the cops who had arrested her when she was seventeen, high as a kite, selling herself at a biker bar. It could have been, but she didn't think so.

She had nearly placed where she knew him from when the fat, slovenly man burst into the bar with the gun and shot the poor bastard at the other side of the diner.

Part V
The Businessman

Daniel tackled the fat murderer with voracity. He felt the fat man grunt and immediately collapse, and he knew right away he would win the fight. What he didn't know was that the gay college guy would see the gun he'd hidden in his belt.

When the two men hit the floor, Daniel ground his knees into the fat man's ass and pushed his face against the linoleum. Daniel grabbed the gun and ripped it out of the fat man's hands. He was about to stand and look at Mary to see how she was doing, but before he could, he felt a hand rip his gun out of his beltline. Shortly after he felt the cold touch of steel against the back of his head.

"You drop that gun now, mister!" The gay boy's voice cracked, and Daniel thought it endearing how hard he was trying to hide his lisp.

Daniel thought back on his night and then took a quick peek at Mary. He saw the fire in her eyes and knew that she was a fighter just as much as he knew that the gun the gay boy was holding was near empty from the night's escapades. He managed a quick glance at the waitress and saw that she was standing in the archway to the kitchen, watching the action. *That's good,* he thought, *at least she hasn't called the cops yet.*

"I mean it, mister!" The crack in his voice was gone, and there was a distinct click of the hammer being drawn back on Daniel's Colt Python. *I guess I underestimated him. This kid has balls.*

Thoughts of Mary's life floated around his mind as he weighed his options. The gay boy was holding a gun that had killed six people. Daniel had killed without remorse and without regret, and now that gun was turned on him. Maybe it was karma; maybe it was cosmic Darwinism.

"Pull the trigger, you fucking fairy." He said it slowly, clearly, and low, almost growling it.

"What?" The weight of the gun against his head abated a bit as the gay boy hesitated in shock.

"I said pull it. You think it matters at this point?" He

looked pointedly at Mary, who stared back at him with desire, an emotion he mistook for love.

Ten years ago Petunia Higgins had sent him a note saying she had been pregnant and had given birth to a beautiful baby girl. Of course by this point, Mary Higgins had already turned eight and had a number of surrogate fathers.

It surprised Daniel to hear that he had a daughter, and he made a decision in that moment to be the best father he could be. The very next day after he got the letter from Petunia, he packed a bag and traveled back from his job in New York to his home state of Wyoming. This would be his penance; this would be his retribution.

His whole life he'd had a terrible temper. He turned to sports as a child to facilitate release of his pent-up emotions, but it only worked for a time. He joined the football team when he entered high school and took up with the in crowd of jocks and cheerleaders. Drugs, steroids, and the untouchable quality of the football greats galvanized his young emotions; he began to get into fights and had trouble with the authorities at school.

It wasn't until the "event" happened during his senior year that he decided it was time for a change. He was with the center of the offensive line and one of the defensive backs, hiding out by the boathouse at the side of the lake. They were giving each other steroid boosters and cocaine bumps when a car pulled up to the woods with a freshman from the school and his little girlfriend.

Deciding that a freshman shouldn't be getting any

more action than they were, they opened the door to the car. The scrawny kid was immediately offended and turned in his seat.

"What the fuck, man! Get outta here!" He seemed to have a Texan drawl.

Daniel stood behind Frank (the center) and Carlos (the defensive back), as they hulked over the open door, peering in on the couple, not saying a thing. The cocaine made them jittery and excited, and the steroids made them quick-tempered.

"I said get the fuck outta here!" the freshman yelled again, trying to grab for the door. The kid was joined soon after by his little girlfriend: "Yeah, you fat fucks!"

When looking back on the incident, Daniel rationalized that the girl mouthing off had caused it, but in actuality the outcome probably would have been the same whether she had said anything or not. The football players never noticed the bumper sticker with the Vagabond biker gang logo on it.

Without saying a word Frank grabbed the girl by her hair and tore her out of the car, clear of the freshman's arms, while Carlos reared back and gave the boy a devastating right hook.

"You shouldn't be with a little prick like that. You should be with a big prick like this." Frank unzipped his fly and pushed his penis in the girl's face.

She squirmed and squeaked while Carlos blocked the freshman's view and continued to pummel him. Daniel stood in the back, vaguely exhilarated, and waited his turn. When Frank was finished, the girl's nose was broken, her dress was torn, and she was no longer a virgin. Then Daniel had his way. Carlos continued to beat the freshman, whose squirming began to slow.

When it came to Carlos's turn he grabbed the girl's throat and squeezed until the girl turned blue. It wasn't until they had put their pants back on that they realized what they had done. Daniel looked in on the destroyed face of the freshman while Frank checked the girl's pulse.

Those were the first two deaths Daniel had experienced. They dumped the bodies in the lake, made promises that they would never talk about the incident again, and parted ways. In the thirty years since, he had been questioned once about the incident, but the bodies were never found.

Coming back to Wyoming brought the memories back to him, as well as the one time he'd had sex with Petunia. It was short and angry, and he never talked to her again. The only correspondence he had with her was the letter he got telling him he was a father of an eight-year-old girl.

Daniel showed up at her school and watched her play on the playground. He felt old anger well up at Petunia for holding this little girl a secret for so long.

She was a beautiful little girl. She was everything he could have hoped for, a small, lithe, spindly little girl with a kind smile. She roamed the playground, dancing around the other children with that broad, kind smile on her face. She laughed and played with both the boys and girls alike, and he felt immense pride well up inside him as tears began to spill from his eyes.

This beautiful young girl was his. He was her father.

He waited until some of the other little ones started to leave, and he waved for her to come over to him. She noticed immediately and waved, giving him that award-winning smile.

His heart warmed with every step she took toward him, his little girl, and she was so beautiful and innocent. He felt himself smiling uncontrollably.

"Hi, mister. My name's Mary." He wanted to pinch her cute little chubby cheeks but kept his hands in his jacket pockets.

"Hi, Mary. D'you know who I am?" He leaned down to her and managed to hold his hand out for her to shake.

"Nooo," she drew out the *o* coyly, "but my stepdaddy says that if a man comes up to me I should play with his pee pee, and he'll give me money for our rent. Is that true?" She continued smiling at him. Daniel went pale and immediately felt sick.

"No. Never talk to any man who may come up to you. Don't listen to anything your stepdaddy says." He wanted to be kind and helpful, but he couldn't help the anger boil up in his stomach. He had images in his head of strangling the man who had misled her so badly.

"'Kay!" She gave him one last smile and turned to continue playing, oblivious to his anger and the implications of her statement.

That night Daniel stood outside Petunia and Mary's house and waited for them to sleep. He watched the drunken slob who was married to Petunia drink and watch TV and eventually pass out on the couch, and then Daniel slowly slipped into the doorway of the trailer. He saw the fat face of the man and the stains on his wifebeater and immediately knew he had to die. He could see in the sleeping slob's face that what Mary had told him was the truth.

He took a blanket from the floor next to the couch and gently squeezed the fat man's nose while covering his mouth. Daniel stood rigid in position for nearly five minutes making sure the fat man didn't stir and then stole his way into Mary's room. She slept on beer- and cum-stained blankets, so Daniel covered her in the blanket that he had used to murder her stepfather. He was careful not to touch her, as if the stain of murder would rub off from his hands and taint her innocent soul.

The rest of the night he spent burying the fat man out next to Lake Meneloua, exactly fifty paces from the boathouse.

He promised himself he wouldn't revisit the grave, and for years he stayed true to his intentions. Petunia would occasionally have a difficult new "stepfather," but Daniel would have a talk with the man, and they always went away. Then Mary turned sixteen and suddenly adopted the moniker Candy. When she was supposed to be out with her friends she was actually prostituting herself out by the biker bars.

Daniel kept his distance and tried not to interfere, but as she got older she got into more and more precarious situations. The more danger she got into, the more he felt he had to be there to protect her. It got to the point where his ventures out to protect his daughter started to interfere with his work, but he couldn't bear to be apart from her. He was always standing in the background, a guardian angel hidden from the fray. Whenever someone got rough with her, he would step in and make sure that man could never hurt her again.

It was only when he was burying his sixth body that he felt he was venturing into dangerous territory. He was standing deep in his mass grave, fifty paces from the boathouse, and looked around at the bodies in varying states of decomposition. *This can't be considered heroic anymore,* he thought. It had never dawned on him that murder, even to protect a family member, was still murder.

Mary was approached by the police twice. The first time was to arrest her for the murders of some of her known johns who had ended up dead. They let her go for a bail of six thousand dollars for prostitution, and she was acquitted of the murder charges. Daniel paid—anonymously, of course. The second time she was arrested, it was in a bar called Stephanie's that was being raided by the ATF. The local police grabbed her up again on prostitution charges. The ATF let her go because it was obvious to them that she was oblivious of the Vagabonds's influence in the bar and of their illegal trafficking.

Two bodies and two years later "Candy" got a call from an introverted disaster of a man. Daniel listened in on the tapped phone conversation in a room he rented in an in-law up the street. He tracked the call (with the machinery he purchased with money from the bank account he called the Good Daddy Fund) and went to the john's house and surveyed who would be taking out his daughter.

What he saw horrified him.

Behind the closed doors that constituted the façade of an office was a room dedicated to murder. There were pictures on the wall of dead women and posted next to their destroyed bodies were newspaper clippings of their young faces declaring them missing. Nazi paraphernalia littered the walls in between the dead women, and two German pistols were carelessly thrown on the desk; but what held the room together was a big tapestry with the sign of the biker gang, the Vagabonds. Daniel stayed in this room for only a moment, and then he pulled out an electronic device and began to study it. A few months earlier he had momentarily borrowed Mary's purse while she was with one of her johns and sewed in a tracking bug, purchased of course with money from the Good Daddy Fund.

He followed the signal for hours until it finally stopped at Lake Meneloua. Daniel smiled when he noticed where the little beacon stopped. It was like divine providence. His prey was going to his burial ground.

When he reached the lake, he parked his car on the

side of the road and walked to the boathouse. He knew the area, he understood the land, and he knew where they were going to go. He was destined to be a hero. Perhaps this was how he was going to introduce himself to his daughter. He was a hero who would catch a mass murderer. He was so lost in his thoughts that by the time he reached the scene, the john had already knocked her against the window and was starting to tear her clothes off.

Daniel, forgetting his desire to be a hero, let his terrifying anger take over. His eyes glazed over, and he pulled out his Colt Python and pulled open the car door. The man in the car was salivating, and his eyes were dilated. When he looked up, Daniel pistol-whipped him as hard as he could. The john screamed and covered his spurting nose, but Daniel didn't hesitate. He grabbed the john by his collar and yanked him out of the car, slamming the man's head into the car door on the way out. The john screamed again, this time in frustration, but he was cut short by the echo of the Python in the open air above Lake Meneloua. Two shots followed in quick succession and then the air over the waters was still again.

Daniel took time to put on gloves and then took care to replace as many of Mary's clothes as he could. He was careful not to touch her, just knowing that the act would wipe off onto her innocent form. He put Mary in his car and drove her back to the interstate. He left her money and left her unmolested and then went back to work on the john. He wanted to keep her away from the knowledge that he was helping her. He was just her guardian angel in the shadows. He wanted her to know her father, not the creature of the night he had become.

He dragged the body behind the boathouse and began digging. Delusions of grandeur raced through his head, how heroic it was, how good a father he was. Pride welled in his chest, and he felt good about his actions, slowly moving aside the bones that were so carefully laid out in his mass grave.

What he didn't notice was the policeman who had spotted his parked Rover and was slowly approaching him.

He later rationalized his actions by telling himself he had done what he had to do. He needed to be a good father. He had to protect his Mary.

When the policemen approached him and asked what he was doing (after he had delicately put the fresh body into the hole), he didn't hesitate. Daniel knew the policeman genuinely didn't know what he was doing; but his natural instincts took over, and he fired two shots from his powerful Python. The officer dropped immediately.

What do I do now? he thought. *They'll know he was out here. They'll know he saw my car. Mary is still lying on the road out there. What if they take her in again? I have to get to Mary!*

Daniel went back to his car and took up the tracker. The blip was moving. She had found another ride. He raced back to his car, ignoring the dull pain in his muscles from burying the two bodies. This was going to be an adventurous night it seemed, and he only had three more bullets in his gun. Then the blip stopped moving.

He noticed two things when he got to Raven's. The first was the raven that sat on the warm neon sign, cawing at him, and the second thing was the coat of arms that hung above the bar. It was the symbol for the Vagabonds.

He made eye contact with the man who was sitting with Mary in a booth. He was a dirty man with long hair. The man smiled and winked ever so slightly. Storm clouds echoed above the diner. The cawing of the crow, two distinct caws, not only warned him he was entering the end of his days but also reminded him how many bullets remained in his Python. He gazed out into the stormy night and on the horizon he saw a distinct separation between the edge of the world and the entrance of the heavens. He hoped Mary's luck kept. He hoped he'd have enough bullets. He looked at the painting over the bar and took a deep breath. Then he looked down at the man sitting with his daughter, a man he knew had brought her here for a purpose, a man who knew Daniel had killed one of his fraternal brothers tonight. *Don't worry, Mary,* he thought. *Your father is here.*

Part VI
The Slob

The power of the gun shocked him. Frank had seen many movies, and in every one the guy with the gun shot smoothly and without remorse. When Frank did it, his arm shook, and brains splattered his face. It shocked and surprised him long enough for him to reconsider whether this was a good idea or not. It wasn't nearly as satisfying as he had thought it would be, and then he was lying on the ground with a businessman playing hero and a young college guy trying to be the bigger hero.

Frank cursed his luck, something that he was very good at, and whimpered at the feel of the gun being pressed against the back of his head.

"Please don't shoot me!" he cried. Both the businessman and the jock turned to look at him, but Frank was looking at the other jock, the one with the accent.

"Please! I'm sorry! I don't want the money anymore! I didn't mean to kill him, I swear! You can keep the money!"

A week earlier Frank had received a phone call, a fortuitous one at that. He was down on his luck again, living in a cockroach-infested shack, late on his rent, and without any prospects of a job. He had beer cans and empty pizza boxes splayed throughout his apartment, creating ragged landscapes of waste. The dust was layered into a thick film, giving his place a slight eggshell hue.

"Franklin Peter Delamotte?" The voice on the other end of the phone had a slight Southern accent, but it was rough around the edges, as if the person speaking was *trying* to be suspicious.

"Speaking."

"I have a proposition for you."

Frank said nothing in response, but he *did* lean forward in his seat. This was something important. *No one* called him by his full name. Not even his mother.

"I'm taking your silence as consent to continue. Today is your lucky day, Franklin. I plan on giving you ten thousand dollars."

Frank continued his silence, more out of shock than contemplation. Ten thousand dollars was a lot of money, and he hadn't paid rent for the last two months. He was surprised he hadn't heard from his landlord yet.

"In return, Mr. Delamotte, I ask a favor from you." The man's drawl changed it to *faaay-va*. Again Frank kept his mouth shut. He missed that the voice had switched into professional diction by using his surname. "At this time, I would in fact, need ya to agree. It's important."

Frank rubbed his face vigorously while trying to decide what to do, but the man on the other end didn't have the patience for it.

"Mista Delamotte. I need you to agree, or you will lose this opportunity. Now, do you agree?"

Frank quickly eyed his studio and assessed the filth, the size, and the smell before he answered.

"Okay, what is it?" His slightly alcoholic drawl taunted the Southern one on the other end.

"Good. Now, Franklin, you will receive your money when you have succeeded in this favor. You will go to the city of Cheyenne, Wyoming, to a place called Raven's Diner. There will be a group of people in the diner, specifically, a man and a woman sitting together. The man may have a ring. You will go on March 15, 2005. There will be a gun strapped behind the broken neon sign. Shoot the man who may or may not have the ring. Then shoot the prostitute. Once this is done, drop the gun and walk out of the diner. When you get back to your studio, your back rent will be paid, and there will be ten thousand dollars waiting for you in a sack just inside ya door." It came out *doe-wa*.

"Right." It was a question more than a statement, drawn out like a groan—*riiiight*—but the man must have picked up on his incredulity, so he continued.

"Mista Delamotte, two shots and walk. Easy money *and* your back rent. Now you have entered into a binding agreement. You cannot back out."

Frank rubbed his chin and quickly looked out the window, feeling eyes on the back of his head.

"Is this some kind of joke?"

"Hardly. Ten thousand dollars plus a pass out of debt. Now before I end this conversation I need to hear some confidence."

"How do I know?" He was talking to buy himself some time, but he was too drunk to think of a plan.

"Mista Delamotte, you disappoint me. If you must have verification, please drive to Breakneck Bend on Mustang Avenue. We will give you half the money now, and we are sure that the money will make all doubt vanish."

Frank tried to say something back, but he heard the dial tone droning, cold and empty in his ear.

He looked about his apartment. The carpet was buried underneath the aggregate filth of years and what he could see was bug-infested.

Ten thousand dollars.

Frank resolved to find out what was in the dark, forest-covered bend on the empty Mustang Avenue.

Mustang Avenue was a dark mysterious expanse of road, which had one particularly dreary and dangerous sharp curve shrouded in shade from the overhanging maples. There was a wall on the edge of the three-foot shoulder, but no reflectors adorned this dark wooden railing. The use of headlights was the law on this dark stretch of road but one that few ever adhered to.

Frank saw the curve up ahead and frowned, trying to mask his fear. He clicked off the radio, distracted by the Boss's rendition of "Nothing Man," and peered out over his dusty dashboard. Seeing nothing, he flicked on his headlights, not out of duty to the law, but out of a sick curiosity for what he might find out there in the shadowy darkness.

A few hundred feet from the curve, he saw a man walking a dog. The man was dressed in black, and the dog was as well. *This must be it*, he thought and parked his car off the shoulder just before the curve. The man paid no attention to him until Frank was near enough to touch him. Then the man spoke.

"There is a man who will be driving through here shortly. He is the one you are to shoot in the diner. The prostitute will be obvious. For now you are to take this dog to the Dumpster at the rear of Raven's Diner and replace it with the duffel bag which will hold the money."

The man never turned to look at him; he just kept his attention on the English bulldog while it did its business.

"What is this? Why did you call me?"

The man turned to Frank with his piercing green-eyed stare.

"You're a poor slob. You need the money. You have nothing to lose. You are the perfect choice. Now, do you understand the instructions I have given you?"

Frank, incredulous at the man's statements, merely nodded.

"Good, the car is a mile down the road. You better get moving." The man produced a gun from his jacket and shot the dog in one fluid motion. Frank took a step back in horror as the man quickly hid the gun and walked straight into the forest.

"What the fuck!" Frank said under his breath and turned to look after the man. But the shadows were thick, and the man had already disappeared into the night.

Frank's heart pounded, bringing bile up to the back of his throat. He looked down and saw that his pants were covered in the blood of the dog, and he wiped at it frantically, trying to disavow the knowledge of what had just happened. The dog's corpse was laying at the edge of the road, and from Frank's point of view it looked serene.

"Could it have been staged?" he wondered out loud, his jowls shaking. It looked like the dog was just lying down on the ground sleeping. Could it be that they had trained the dog to play dead at the sound of the gun? Frank wondered how they had gotten the blood to splatter on his pants. He couldn't see any blood on the dog.

Frank boldly walked over to the creature, angry that these people thought him stupid enough to fall for a cheap parlor trick, but when he got within reach, he recoiled and retched on the side of the road.

The side of the dog's head had been blown away, and Frank hadn't noticed the small black hole just above its collar.

Desperately Frank grasped at its hind legs, trying to stay clean. Looking back at his car, he cursed himself for parking so far away and then began to drag the dog back to his car. He nearly got there, too.

He was passing the rear driver's-side door when he saw the headlights of another car moving around the curve.

Shit! he thought. *The person driving is going to see me dragging a dog with half a head!* He did the first thing that came to him.

He dropped the dog and quickly started walking toward the headlights. *With any luck they'll just drive right past me.* He took a few steps forward, praying for the best, but when the car got near, it began to slow. *Keep going, keep going.* But the car continued to slow until it seemed to be just crawling toward him. *Fucking Good Samaritan.* But then he remembered something the informant had said. The man he was supposed to shoot was going to be in a car that would drive by.

He squinted and covered his eyes with one hand, cursing the man for not leaving the gun he had shot the dog with. This could be all over now. *Ten thousand dollars!*

He stood tall and tried as best he could to hide the dog behind him as the car slowly rolled up to him.

"Howdy! Having some car trouble?" the man asked. Frank could tell the man was white, but the car was veiled in shadows. Frank didn't answer him, just continued to sneer, trying to decipher more specifics about the man.

"You hear me, man?" Frank heard the concern in the man's voice and relished it. He knew he should say something to make the man feel more at ease. Hell, maybe he could kill him here and now, and everything would be resolved without any shooting later in the diner. The only thing that held him back was something the Southern man on the phone had told him. *Shoot the man who may or may not have the ring. Then shoot the prostitute.*

The car was near enough for Frank to get a decent glimpse of the man before, presumably, the man saw the dog lying behind him and possibly the blood spatter on his trousers. Frank took a step toward him, arms outstretched, still with no exact expression on his face and still without saying anything. The man's eyes bulged, and the car suddenly jumped forward and zoomed down the road.

Frank chuckled as the exhaust swirled around him. There had been a stack of papers in the passenger seat. On top of the stack of papers was what looked like a title page. It said, "Down on Luck by Robert Tanner."

Frank took his time loading the dog into the car, but he was long gone before the police arrived on the scene. He chuckled the whole way to Raven's Diner, thinking about the ten thousand dollars and how he would spend it.

Part VII
The Encounter

"I'm sorry. I know I was supposed to shoot her, too. But I didn't mean to kill him, and it kinda shocked me. It was like the dog. There's just so much blood." Dark stains began to spread across the taut fabric at his armpits, and a sour odor emanated from his perspiring body. "Please, I just want to go!"

"What the hell are you talking about?" A new emotion crept across Daniel's face as he spoke—fear.

His voice was nearly drowned out by Tanya's screaming. She didn't take notice of the others in the room. She slipped out of the seat and cradled Robert's head in her arms. Blood covered her, mixed with the surprisingly white bone fragments from his skull. She tried to fix the wound, pushing the bone back against his head, until she realized how futile her efforts were.

She felt as if something wasn't right in the world. *This wasn't supposed to happen. He wasn't supposed to die that easily. He took care of Chopper single-handedly. How could this happen? It can't be true!*

She combed his hair back from his face and kissed his forehead while periodically shaking his head.

"What's he talking about?" the businessman said to the jock still sitting in the booth, ignoring the gun at the back of his head.

Charles sat silent by the table. All he could think about was the note. Someone here knew they had killed the girl; however, none of them looked like the man in the white suit. He knew the businessman was yelling at him, but he couldn't process the situation. Was the robber just happenstance? Would there be someone else coming in through the door to deal with him? Or was it the slob?

"Why did you want him to shoot Mary?" Daniel roared at Charles. Daniel forgot all about the slob bawling on the ground and turned his attention to Charles. The boy was looking down at Daniel, and his eyes were full of fear. Something more was going on than met the eye. *The kid who's holding the gun came here with the kid the shooter is talking to.*

"What is he talking about?" Daniel asked Abe, indicating Charles with the gun. Frank was now a crying mess on the ground.

Abe was astonished. He still held the gun to Daniel, but Daniel was acting as if all was well. Then Abe remembered what Charles had told him about the man with the letter. He thought about what they had done and why they were there. He looked into the fire of Daniel's eyes and felt all the courage in his body evaporate. This was a man who had no qualms about killing. He had a way of looking at a person, as if he were looking right through him. Abe shivered and shook his head. He wanted to say something but was worried how it was going to come out.

Daniel thanked God that Tanya had stopped screaming; he might have a chance to think. He knew he couldn't stay there. An unregistered gun that had killed eight people wasn't the greatest thing to have on you during a police interrogation. He tried to piece together the puzzle forming in his head: This slob comes in and shoots a man, and then later says he didn't mean to kill him. He insinuates that a college kid put him up to it, paying him an as-yet-undisclosed sum of money; and for some reason that same person wants to shoot Mary.

Daniel slapped the gun in Abe's hand to the side. A smile touched his lips when the boy pulled the trigger, sending the bullet wide. He raised his gun, pressing the barrel into Abe's head, and then turned to look at Charles.

"What the fuck is he talking about, boy?"

"Please." Abe whimpered, crossing his eyes to look at the barrel. Charles didn't answer.

"It was you, right? The accent?" Frank muttered on the ground, desperately trying to get an answer from Charles. Charles stared at Abe.

"I don't have time for this." Daniel's famous anger was noticeable in his voice. "One more time, boy. What's going on?" Abe let out a moan, and Frank loudly farted.

Charles still said nothing, staring wide-eyed at the gun in Daniel's hand.

Tanya, meanwhile, had let go of her vise grip on

Robert's head and in doing so lost her grip on reality. Her vision turned red, and black spots invaded her peripheral vision. She quietly stood and grabbed a steak knife from the table while the men were arguing. She took a look over at Mary who was crouched in a booth hiding her face and felt the anger renew, white flashes spotting her already diminished vision. *He should have shot you first, bitch.*

There was a loud resounding bang as Daniel pulled the trigger. Abe fell back to the ground, lifeless. Then Daniel turned his gun to Charles.

"What exactly did he tell you, and how do you know it was him?" Daniel asked Frank, while looking at Charles. Frank, confused and terrified, stared at Abe's corpse and held his breath. He didn't answer, and he didn't hear Tanya approaching from behind him.

"*You*, slob. I'm talking to *you*." Daniel tore his gaze away from Charles and looked down at Frank.

"Stop!" Daniel yelled, surprised that Tanya had gotten as close to Frank as she had. She was holding the blade overhand above her head. Daniel swung his gun around to stop her, but he was too late.

There was a sickening crunch as the blade hit the top of Frank's head and then a loud grinding noise as the blade slid down the front of his face and buried itself into his windpipe.

Daniel pulled the trigger on Frank's Glock, and Tanya's head popped backward, sending her slumping to the ground. He cursed himself for forgetting the grieving woman, but he was thankful to her for making the shot easy. He knew he would have had to kill her anyway. If he was going to get away, there could be no witnesses to the events of that night.

He had begun to turn back to Charles when he heard Mary cry out. He whirled around and saw Charles holding Mary by her beautiful hair, pressing Frank's Python to her head.

"Y-you d-drop that thing now, mista!" Charles stuttered, his Southern accent still prevalent. Mary looked Daniel in the eye, and he could see the little girl in her.

"Hhhelp." Frank's voice came out bubbly and grating, as if he was choking.

Daniel ignored Frank and looked at Charles. Inwardly he cursed himself again. He should not have walked into this environment—simply too many variables. Now he had to protect Mary and get her out of there but make sure no one else did. *Shit, there's still the waitress*, he thought. He did not divert his attention, though; some things were of a higher priority.

"Things may have gotten a little out of hand, boy. Death can do that. Now just tell me. What is this slob talking about? Why is he apologizing to you?" He adjusted his grip on the pistol and flexed his arm. He had to move fast, and he had to be accurate—one shot to the head hiding behind his beloved daughter.

"I dunna what's going on! You just let me go, ya hear?" There was a rustle from the kitchen, but Daniel decided he needed to take his shot and then deal with whatever was going on out there. The police were probably almost there, and he needed to move fast if he was going to get away. He would have to forgo the information he was seeking.

"Don't lie to me," Daniel said as calmly as he could muster.

"I ain't lying! I …" While Charles muttered, Daniel turned his head toward the kitchen, gasping, as if someone was barging into the room, all the while keeping Charles in his peripheral vision.

When Charles turned to see what Daniel was looking at, Daniel took his shot, quickly raising the gun and taking short aim. Charles fell limply away from Mary, and Daniel lithely moved forward, cradling Mary in his arms. He kissed her on the forehead and felt tears well up in his eyes. It was the first time he'd ever touched her.

"I was hoping it was going to be you." The voice came from the kitchen and echoed in the small, bloody room. Daniel turned to see who was speaking, but before he could he felt electricity enter his body from the sting of a taser. The ledge of reality he had been struggling to hold on to crumbled slowly away … and everything was dark.

Part VIII
Revelations

Mary's screams of agony awoke him. Daniel ached all over, but when he tried to move, he found his arms and legs bound. He slowly opened his eyes, and little by little the darkness receded.

He was in the kitchen of the diner, or at least he assumed it was the diner. Mary was being held over the stove by a tall, burly man. Her face was a collage of burned skin, and each teardrop sizzled on the burner, as if wiping away her right to feel.

"*Stop!*" Daniel yelled through coarse vocal cords. The big man turned to look at him. He had a devilish, angular smile. He let go of Mary, and she fell to the ground, whimpering. Then a voice spoke from behind him.

"Welcome back to the world, Daniel." The voice was distinctly feminine, and the determination in the voice scared him.

"We's just so happy to see ya," the big man said in a fake Southern drawl. Then he giggled. His laugh was high-pitched and sounded like a weasel.

"Leave her alone. She didn't do anything," Daniel attempted. He tried to take a deep breath but felt something constricting his chest.

"You're telling me that a disease-infested whore didn't do anything?" It was a new voice, one that Daniel recognized, but he couldn't quite tell where it had come from.

"You've brought this on yourself, Daniel. You have sinned. You have murdered, and now it's time for your comeuppance." The woman walked into his view, and he immediately recognized her from the outfit she was wearing.

"Do you repent, Daniel?" The waitress's nametag said "Stephanie."

"Quite honestly, I don't give a shit if you repent or not,

but you killed one too many Vagabonds." Daniel finally remembered where he knew the man from; it was the man who had brought Mary here earlier in the evening.

"You see, you did a lot of dirty work for us, Daniel," the man said. "We were gonna kill all those people out there. Then Stephanie here came up with the plan. We lured you all in, and you did the work for us. It was brilliant. Now with the infector over there gone and her benefactor, meaning you, Daniel, out of the way, we bikers can take a breath of fresh air. How many of us did you kill?"

Daniel tried to answer, but he was too short of breath. He looked down and saw a rope tied around his chest. As he watched, he saw it visibly tighten.

"Robert and Tanya only killed Chopper. Charles and Abe killed Kickstand's little girl. Frank was the easy fall guy. And then there are you two." The rope tightened as the man spoke, and Daniel felt his lungs burning. He felt the crack of two of his ribs as the rope cinched tighter. "The pariah and the avenger."

"Your time of destruction is over, Daniel. We will now live in peace." Stephanie smiled down at him and gently caressed his cheek. "Goodbye, Daniel."

The rope tightened again, and the light slowly drained from his vision. *I'll be with you soon, my darling. I'm sorry I couldn't save you in this world, but nothing will touch you in the next.*

"And you, darling. I'm gonna be happy that I will never have to see your face in my bar or my diner ever again." A ghost of a smile played about Stephanie's lips.

CPSIA information can be obtained at www.ICGtesting.com
Printed in the USA
235619LV00001B/67/P